MW00936077

Name & Number

by

John Hoskison

This book is dedicated to the lifer Mike Hart and the guys on 'A' wing for keeping me safe. Without their protection I would not have survived.

Other Titles by John Hoskison

Inside – One Man's Experience of Prison
No Hiding in The Open
A Golf Swing You Can Trust
Lower Your Golf Scores
The Short Game Silver Bullet

A Note from the Author

Dear Reader

There are dangerous men in prison; predators who sniff out the weak. They stalk the dark corridors searching for victims; anything for that extra phone card or packet of 'smack'.

Prisons are full of bad people who've done bad things... They can also become home to people like you and me.

Ever driven a car carelessly and broken the Highway Code? Maybe used your phone on the drive home to say you'll be late for dinner? Or said yes (and knew you shouldn't) to that extra gin and tonic at the staff party?

Every day, normal people take unnecessary risks and break the law. If not you, then it's likely you know someone who does. Most of the time people get away with it. But given the wrong circumstances, jail time can become reality. Unfortunately, it did for me.

After experiencing the horrors of prison, I know how important it is to help keep our young people safe. There are many temptations at schools and universities and we need to guide our sons and daughters away from trouble. Every day I talk to youngsters who have made the wrong call at the wrong time and are facing time behind bars.

Name & Number is about a young man trying to survive the violence and terror in prison. While fictional, it is drawn from my real-life experiences of serving time in some of the toughest prisons in Britain; places of medieval-like squalor and violence.

If you know anyone who's under the impression that 'it could never happen to me', this book is worth a read. Maybe it'll make them think twice before taking a risk that will turn their life upside down.

Chapter 1

Nick Wood sat with his back pressed hard against the seat of the van. He rolled his neck and tried to ease his shoulders. Even though he was small, the cage he was locked into was a tight fit and with little ventilation the heat was stifling. Perspiration trickled down his back. He wiped his forehead with the back of his hand. Now he knew why it was called a 'sweat box'.

Along with three other prisoners Nick was being transported from court to Her Majesty's Prison Blackthorpe. He turned his head towards the window and gazed out at the passing view. Rain had given way to a clear sky and the sun was now shimmering on the autumn leaves that covered the wayside. In other circumstances he would have appreciated the scenery, but not now. He closed his eyes tight and tried to blot out memories of his morning in court, but nightmare images kept flashing through his mind; the stern face of the judge, the surly guards, his mother and sister both looking tense and scared. He wondered how his mother was coping. 'You'll be the death of me!' she'd yelled at him the night he was arrested, but she'd soon calmed down and sorted out the practical side of things; like talking to his tutors at college and finding him a decent lawyer.

She'd been really brave, even when the barrister had warned them that he might get six months. But today in court when the judge had read out his sentence, Nick couldn't help but glance up to where she sat. Her face was deathly pale and he could tell she was trying not to cry. It was moments later that he heard her break down. It had taken a few seconds for the judge's words to sink in.

'Two years,' rang through Nick's head. Two

years for doing what a dozen others at his college were doing... but they hadn't had his rotten luck. He immediately thought of
Jessica and what had happened to her. No doubt her parents would consider his sentence not nearly long enough.

Nick gripped the side of his seat as the van gained pace. The driver seemed in a hurry and the vehicle swayed from side to side as they sped along the road. Locked away in his small compartment Nick couldn't see the other inmates but he'd met them when they were waiting to board the van. The two men opposite him were both older than he was, in their late twenties he guessed and both looked pretty mean. The man locked in the cage in front of him had a thick jagged scar across his face and looked like he belonged in a horror film. A conversation had started up between the three while they were waiting to board. 'Hey Scarface,' one of them had called out. 'How long you doing this time?'

'Five stretch. Some wanker tried to sell gear on my patch—had to sort him out!'

'You still on the drugs?'

'What do you fuckin' wanna know for?' said Scarface.

'There's meant to be a grass in the nick we're going to,' said the man. 'Gonna have to watch your back if you're on the gear'.

'Did you hear what we did to the grass in Coldash?' said Scarface.

'Boiling water all over his nuts—nice one'.

'They deserve it,' said Scarface. 'The more painful the better. Got some new tricks for any grass we catch.'

Nick had listened with an increasing sense of dread. He'd cringed at the thought of anyone having boiling water poured over them and it sounded like

Scarface had worse up his sleeve. As the van made its way towards their new prison, Nick folded his arms tightly across his chest and tried to reassure himself. I can't be locked up with this lot he decided.

Throughout the months awaiting trial he'd avoided thinking about prison. He'd just read one article. 'Take a look at this,' his mother had said. 'It's about a new prison.' According to the paper a golf course was being planned for a prison that already had a swimming pool and a state-of-the-art gym. On the same page was a letter from a member of parliament saying what a disgrace it was that prisoners were treated better than pensioners. 'Nice one. If I do get sent to jail let's hope I get sent there,' Nick had said to his mum trying to put a brave face on it, but in reality the thought of any prison terrified him.

The van slowed down, turned off the main road and headed down a narrow country lane. The sunlight was fading fast. His mum and Lisa, his kid sister, would be back home by now. He couldn't help wondering if his dad would phone them to find out how it went. He definitely wasn't in court. Nick's eyes had scanned the room to see if his old man had turned up. He was neither surprised nor disappointed to see that he wasn't there. Nothing his dad did or didn't do surprised him—not after the way he'd walked out on them two years before. He'd left to set up home with Carine, his hairstylist; a girl the same age as Nick, just turned nineteen. There had been some terrible rows and Nick and his sister had kept out of the way. His mother had sobbed for days after he left and Nick had tried to comfort her the best he could. 'We don't need him, mum,' he'd said. 'We can cope without him.' He wondered what Lisa would say to comfort his mum today. Would she say the same about Nick? Would she tell her mum that they were better off without him?

Out of the window a sign suddenly caught his attention—NEXT LEFT—HMP BLACKTHORPE.

Nick felt sick as he set eyes on the prison. Even if the sun had still been shining it would have looked a formidable sight. Barbed wire sat on top of the high walls and there were security cameras everywhere. Behind the walls loomed a vast grey building with hundreds of small windows, but there was no sign of life. Nick had seen similar scenes to this before—from the safety of a cinema seat where he'd enjoyed watching American films about the hostile life in a state penitentiary.

The van slowed as it headed towards the main gate and the driver sounded the horn. When it came to a complete stop the driver blasted the horn again, but this time the noise re-bounded off the prison walls and came crashing back at the van. With his head pressed hard against the window Nick watched the huge prison gates open. There was a large notice attached to the wall outside and when the van started to move through, Nick tried to read the words but they was covered in grime and he could only make out a few: Treat them with humanity and help them lead law-abiding lives in prison and after release. Nick relaxed slightly, thinking, Well if they're the rules, it can't be all that bad.

The van drove into a large dark hanger, the engine stopped and the driver got out and slammed his door. Then an unnerving silence. For a while all four prisoners sat quietly as if collecting themselves, then all of a sudden, as if ready for battle, Scarface started kicking the door of his cage—Thud!—Thud!— Thud! 'Let us out you bastards!' he roared. His feet lashed out and his fists smashed against the walls. The two other prisoners then began stamping their feet and joined in the chant, 'Screw bastards—let us out!'

Nick couldn't understand why no-one came to stop the noise and he wasn't sure what to do. If he joined in he might get into trouble. If he didn't, the others would think him a wimp. Eventually there was a brief lull as the inmates tired and Nick heard heavy footsteps approach the van. Then all of a sudden— *Thwack!* Nick jumped out of his skin and guessed a guard must have lashed out with his boot at the van from outside.

Keys were then inserted into the lock, the doors opened and a tall thin guard, dressed in a black prison uniform, climbed in 'Right you lot,' he said gesturing aggressively with his head. 'Out you get.'

Nick was last to get off the van and at the top of the steps he hesitated for a quick glimpse of the prison before climbing down. In those brief seconds he was able to see more of HMP Blackthorpe and realised it had nothing in common with the prison he'd read about in his mum's newspaper. It was a concrete jungle. There was no need to look for any signs of recreational activities. There wasn't a blade of grass to be seen, let alone a golf course. Nick followed the others across the yard to where four guards were standing, hands on hips and legs astride. The guards looked pretty tough. Nick guessed they'd have to be to deal with the likes of Scarface, it was the last job he'd have chosen. He just hoped they would realise he'd be causing no trouble and they'd help keep him safe. As he walked towards them he kept his head down and his eyes to the ground.

* * *

From opposite sides of the prison yard, two men watched the arrival of the new inmates. Tom Hawks, serving twenty-five years for armed robbery and murder, watched from his cell on the 'lifer's' wing. Tom had seen the coming and going of prisoners hundreds of times before. Twenty years, two hundred and forty months, or a thought that really depressed Tom, nearly eight thousand days he had now spent behind bars. He smiled ruefully. It would take a better mathematician than himself to calculate the number of hours he had sat alone during that time, regretting the day he had ended up serving life for murder.

Tom studied the new men as they shuffled along to the entrance of the prison block. Sure enough they looked the normal mix of characters, he even recognised one from the old days, but his eye rested on the last one in line. He shook his head. They shouldn't be sending kids to a place like this...

On the opposite side of the prison the other man watched the new recruits with more than idle interest. To 'The Dragon' all four were potential customers— his personal money making machines. He took a deep drag of his joint and didn't flinch as the smoke bit into his lungs. An insect buzzed round his head and came to rest on the red and golden dragon tattooed on his neck. He idly waved it away, his concentration was on the prisoners below. His eyes scanned the line and came to rest on the youngster at the end. What have we got ourselves here then he thought grinning slyly. Looks like I've got myself another mug who'll need protecting. Once more the fly landed on the man's tattoo—this time he crushed it.

* * *

Inside the prison block, Nick stood in line with the other prisoners. Unlike the sweat box the room they were waiting in was freezing. He had heard one of the guards refer to it as the 'reception area' and he wanted to look around but thought better of it. He didn't want to attract anyone's attention.

For a half an hour they stood in line waiting and Nick started to feel hungry. His mum had suggested he eat something at breakfast but he had refused. When she'd put two slices of toast on the table in front of him, as soon as her was back was turned he'd dumped them in the bin. There was no way he could have eaten a thing, he was too nervous, but now he was starving. He rubbed his wrists where earlier handcuffs had chafed his skin and wondered what sort of food, if any, they would be given. From the looks of the reception area, dark and dingy as it was, the prison wouldn't be in any 'Good Food Guide'.

Suddenly a door on the right opened and an officer with a shaved head came into the room. He was a tall tough looking man who, like the other officers Nick had seen, had a thick, black moustache. Nick wondered if it was a compulsory part of a prison officer's uniform. The guard stared down at his clipboard, 'Andrews 438!' he called out. No-one answered and the officer raised his head and voice, 'Don't play silly buggers with me,' he snarled. He repeated the question and this time there was a response from the man standing next to Nick. 'Yeah,' he said casually.

The guard moved towards Andrews, 'Yes—Guv,' he bawled. 'Mess with me 438 and you'll end up down the block.'

Nick didn't know what he meant by 'the block' and by the sound of it he wouldn't want to. When his own name was called out he answered 'Yes Guv,' without hesitating.

The next two hours were a further nightmare when he was led from reception into a smaller room where his photo and fingerprints were taken and entered into the prison records. Then came the medical that was carried out by the prison doctor. 'What about your sex life?' he asked Nick.

'What about it?' said Nick thinking, what's that got to do with anything?

'Do you have a regular girlfriend?'

'No.' He immediately thought of Jessica and that last time in the back of the car.

'Are you gay?'

'What?' Nick said glaring at the doctor. 'No,' he said loudly making sure the others heard. The final insult was when his head was searched for lice after which the doctor handed him a disinfectant body wash and told him to take a shower. After towelling down Nick put on the prison clothes he had been given; a pair of faded denim jeans, a shirt that was two sizes too big and worst of all—a second hand pair of underpants. Nick had always kept himself clean, the thought of wearing somebody else's underwear made him cringe. He was also given a small bag which contained a tooth brush, some soap and toilet paper.

After all the checks had been completed, Nick was led to the far side of the prison and the induction wing where all new inmates were housed. For most of the time he walked in a daze as he followed the others along the dimly lit corridors. With every step he became increasingly depressed. Stripped of everything, including his dignity, he was no longer Nick Wood who had friends and a family and rights. He was now Wood 582—just a name and a number.

At the end of each corridor he was jolted back to reality by the sound of the huge steel doors being opened and shut. As each one crashed back into place it was like another nail being hammered into his coffin. Nick lost count how many they passed through. The only time someone spoke was when they passed a door marked with red lines. Scarface looked back to Nick with an evil grin on his face. 'That leads to the lifer's wing,' he said in a hushed voice.

Nick swallowed hard. 'Are they dangerous?' he asked.

'They'd cut yer throat as soon as look at yer,' said Scarface dramatically drawing a finger across his neck. Nick quickened his pace and caught up with the escorting guard.

'Take no notice of him, he's only trying to wind you up. He's worse than any of them,' he said.

Nick realised the officer was trying to reassure him but his words weren't much comfort. He knew that lifers were only in prison for one thing—murder. If Scarface is worse than any of them he's got to be a complete nightmare, thought Nick. The inmates had been told they would have to share cells due to the overcrowding, so someone was going to have to share with Scarface. Nick closed his eyes and pleaded. Please God—don't let it be me.

As they moved further into the prison Nick stayed close to the officer but kept his eyes to the ground so he could pick a way through the mess. The floor was filthy and strewn with discarded cardboard cups and plates. The other three prisoners swaggered along carelessly kicking the litter out of the way as they went. Nick noticed how at ease they seemed to be. Twice they passed the end of corridors where they saw other prisoners, 'Glad to see you back Andrews—you owe me!' yelled one guy who was carrying a ghetto blaster that was blaring out rap.

'Scarface you bastard—you owe me half an ounce of burn!' shouted another. They all seemed to know each other and Nick started to feel like an alien that had landed on a forbidden planet.

When they finally reached the induction wing Nick looked up in awe—it was massive. Built on three levels, with over fifty cells to a level, it was just like the inside of an old fashioned galleon ship Nick had once seen on television. Through the middle of the building was an iron staircase that spiralled up to the top floor and safety netting stretched across each level to catch anything thrown from the cells. Nick was relieved to see that the prisoners were locked away in their cells, but even so the atmosphere was unnerving. Music blared out and inmates shouted loudly to each other from cell to cell. As they climbed towards the top landing the noise became deafening and Nick began to feel sick with panic. Who was he going to have to share with? Would it be Scarface? Would it be some nutter in for rape?

On the top landing the guard led them between a row of cells until he came to a stop. 'You're in first Wood,' he said selecting a key from his belt and unlocking the heavy steel door. Nick didn't want to move but Scarface gave him a nudge, ''ave fun,' he said winking. It was the moment Nick had dreaded. He hesitated outside the cell; it was dark inside, like a cave. The smell of stale urine assaulted his nostrils. He wanted to turn and run; escape, back to the night his life had been torn apart. He glanced round for help, a sign from the guard that he would be alright, but the guard took hold of his bag of possessions, threw them forward, and pushed him inside.

* * *

On the lifer's wing Tom Hawks rolled himself a cigarette then slid the pouch across the small table towards Winston, his next door neighbour. It was early evening, work had finished for the day and the two men were in Tom's cell playing cards. Tom was feeling thirsty after having had a second helping of the evening meal—over-salted spaghetti mash. 'Spaghetti Bolognesi' the canteen manager had called it and Tom didn't argue. It was a long time since he'd seen and tasted the real thing.

He was about to suggest Winston should make them both a cup of tea when a prison officer knocked and poked his head round the door. Tom grinned at the screw. 'Come for a cuppa, Les?' he said.

'If there's one going.'

The officer sat down on Tom's bed and leaned forward resting his elbows on his knees. His neatly cut hair and trimmed moustache were grey and his nose was red from an over fondness for whisky. With the top half of his right ear missing and a broken nose, Les Wright looked a formidable sight. Tom however had learned how to handle him and considered him a pussy cat. Les had been a serving officer in Her Majesty's Prisons for as long as Tom had been serving his sentence and it was a standing joke, among the two of them, as to who would escape first. Les looked at Winston. 'Nice and hot, there's a good lad.'

Winston took the hint and got up from his chair, 'I'll get them,' he said.

Tom winked at him, 'Good man,' he said, 'take your time we're in no hurry.'

Les took a packet of cigarettes from his pocket and threw one across. 'Thanks,' said Tom as he slipped his tobacco pouch back inside his trousers. He lit the end and inhaled deeply, 'Keep promising myself I'll give them up.'

'Same with me,' said Les, coughing. 'My wife thinks I have, I only smoke at work, not at home.' The word didn't affect Tom. Blackthorpe was the only home he had, but he took another drag and changed the subject. 'What's new then Les?' he asked, knowing that Les liked to gossip.

'Four new inmates came in this afternoon.'

Tom was being told what he already knew. 'Four more, eh? Soon be standing room only.'

'Tell me about it, Tom. We're having to double up in some of the single cells. Huh—Soames was one of them that came in today. Old Scarface. You know him, don't you Tom?'

'Yeah, I shared with him in the Scrubs—a right smack 'ead.'

'Most of them are nowadays.'

'Then why aren't you lot doing something about it?'

'The governor says he's on top of it,' said Les.

Tom shook his head, 'He's on top of it all right—sitting upstairs away from it all. He couldn't give a toss.'

Les didn't comment—he didn't have to. Tom knew how Les felt about their latest governor. Mr Striker was popular with neither the screws nor the inmates. He was on a fast track promotion scheme where statistics meant everything and the welfare of the inmates came last on his list. 'You're not making some poor sod share with Scarface are you, Les?'

'It's like a cattle market over there, Tom. It'll be luck of the draw,' he said shrugging.

Tom thought about the young kid he'd seen arrive. The first two weeks in prison were the hardest—it was the same for everybody. You think there might be time to adjust but everything happens at once; new rules to learn, a new environment to adjust to, a tidal wave of bullying, drugs and violence. Sink or swim time, thought Tom reflecting on the amount of inmates who think about topping themselves during the first fourteen days. If the kid could get through the first two weeks he'd be in with a chance of surviving, thought Tom. One thing was for sure, if he was put in to share with someone half decent it could make all the difference.

At that moment the door pushed open and Winston sauntered in with two mugs of tea. He handed one to Tom and put the other on the table. Les nodded his thanks, picked up his cup and took a sip. There was a moments silence then his face screwed up in disgust, 'Urgh! You can tell this isn't P.G. tips' he said wincing, 'tastes more like gnat's piss.'

Chapter 2

Nick tried to regain his balance after being shoved into the cell but when he turned back towards the door he was already too late—CRASH! Suddenly he was alone with no one to help. For a moment he stood rooted to the spot not daring to move. There was no noise, no sign of any movement. More importantly there was no attack. After a few moments his shoulders started to relax and his eyes became accustomed to the dim light. Slowly he turned round to survey his new home.

The cell was much smaller than he'd imagined and at first no-one else was visible. On the right, up against the wall, was a small table and two scruffy wooden chairs. Next to the table was a dirty looking sink, above it a small window protected with black metal bars. On the left were bunk beds. The top one, Nick quickly realised, was occupied. A pair of feet stuck out from under a prison green blanket but the rest of the inmate was covered. Whoever it was had obviously chosen to ignore the intrusion and Nick wondered what he should do.

He saw his bag on the floor where the guard had tossed it. He bent down, picked it up and was about to sit on one of the chairs when the inmate on the top bunk threw off the blanket and sat up. The sudden movement startled Nick. 'Well, well, looks like I got myself a right result. I won't be the youngest in this shithole any longer,' he said taking in the sight of his new cell mate. 'So, what's your name, then?'

Normally Nick would have tried a friendly smile but he was learning to keep his emotions in check and he answered deadpan. 'Nick—Nick Wood.'

'Nick Wood? Is that what you're in for—nicking wood?' the youth said laughing. Nick managed a wary smile. The young man swung his legs round. 'When they told me I'd gotta share I nearly did me nut,' he said reaching down and holding out his hand, but then mockingly withdrawing it before Nick could shake it. Like a monkey he swung himself down onto the bottom bunk and perched himself on the edge. 'My names Jason Smith,' he said grinning. 'And I nick anything that's goin'.'

Jason Smith was small, about five feet six, thin and pale, so pale that Nick wondered if he was ill. Perhaps he'd been 'inside' for quite some time he thought.

'Sit down—make yourself at home,' said Jason. Nick reached out and took hold of the nearest chair. He sat down taking the weight off his feet and for the first time since entering prison he started to relax. Rather than being banged up with some oversized thug who would terrorise and bully him, he was with someone the same age as himself who appeared no immediate threat. He looked across at Jason who was peering at him intently. As though assessing Nick was ready for interrogation, Jason leaned forward and asked the question all inmates eventually ask their cell mates, 'What you in for then?' he said.

Nick still found it hard to tell anyone what had happened; the reason he was now in prison. 'I was done for supplying drugs,' he said quietly.

'Cool,' said Jason, a grin lighting up his face, 'Got any on you now?'

'No. I'm not into drugs,' said Nick.

'Yeah right,' said Jason smirking.

'I'm not. It was a one off. I was given a few 'E's to sell at a party as a favour for a friend. I was caught in possession.'

'Is that it?' said Jason clearly disappointed. 'How long you doin' then?'

'Two years.' said Nick.

'Two years for sellin' a few 'E's? There's gotta be more to it than that.' Nick's mind went back to when Jessica had collapsed in the night club. He remembered how helpless he'd felt, and the sheer terror when he found out she was in a coma. Nick looked at Jason, 'My girlfriend took one of them. She collapsed and was rushed to hospital into intensive care.'

Jason let out a whistle. 'Bad luck mate. Bet that shit you up.'

An imaginary picture of Jessica on a life support machine came into Nick's mind. He hadn't been allowed to see her. Her father had sent a message to Nick telling him to stay away from the bedside or he'd kill him. The threat hadn't bothered Nick, he'd wanted to die. But then, in the cell, he felt the familiar surge of relief he first experienced when he had found out she was going to survive. He looked up at Jason. 'She pulled through,' he said. 'She's all right now.'

'Just as well for you she is mate or you'd 'ave been banged up for manslaughter, huh, only two years? With my record, I'd 'ave got six.'

Nick watched his cell mate casually roll up a cigarette and wondered what he'd been up to in the past. 'What are you in for, Jason?' he asked tentatively. 'What have you done?'

Jason took a long drag on his fag, threw his head back and blew smoke rings into the air. 'Easier to ask me what I 'aven't done.'

Looking at his build Nick decided Jason could be a cat burglar. He was the right size and certainly agile enough. Nick imagined him shinning up drain pipes and clambering across roof tops.

'It was the fuckin' cameras that got me,' said Jason. 'Hadn't been for them I'd 'ave got away with it. Instead I've got eighteen months in this shithole.'

'Are you a burglar then?' Nick asked.

'Burglar? Do I look like a burglar?' Jason leaned back and lifted his legs up on the bunk. 'I burgled me first house at the age of five. Served me apprenticeship with me old man. He was the best.'

'Was?' said Nick. 'Is he dead now?'

'Dead? No. He's over the water.'

'What? You mean America?'

'Jesus—you are fuckin' green. He's on the Isle of White—doin' a ten stretch in Albany.' Jason got up off the bed and from behind one of the chairs he pulled out a bucket, undid his flies and started to urinate. Nick looked on astonished. 'There's no bogs in the cells,' said Jason. 'You wanna have a slash you piss in this. At night if you wanna go for a crap you can push the button on the wall. If you're lucky the door unlocks for about five minutes—but sometimes it doesn't. Make sure you empty this in the morning or it stinks. Got it?' he asked. Nick nodded, now understanding why the cell smelt of stale urine.

Jason zipped up his flies and moved towards the cell door, 'I've gotta go,' he said.

'Go where?' Nick asked thinking that the cell door was locked.

Jason put his hand on the handle, pushed and suddenly lights from the landing outside flooded the cell.

'Fuck' said Nick in surprise. He had been told during his reception talk that the cell doors were operated by an electronic system. They were unlocked at five o'clock in the afternoon for tea, and at seven o'clock in the morning for breakfast and work. He presumed that when inmates were in their cells the doors would be locked.

Jason turned round and grinned. 'Thought we were all safe and tucked up in 'ere did you?' he chided. 'The doors are left open most of the time unless you go to work. Depends which screw's on duty. Only time you're safe in 'ere's at night after bang up. He turned round and took a peek outside. 'Right I've gotta go.'

'Where?' asked Nick anxious not to be left alone.

'Bit nosey aren't you?' Jason said glancing round.

'Sorry—I just wondered what I do now?'

'Go get your tea, I'll be back for bang up at eight, then it's lights out at ten. Same as any day in 'ere.' Jason turned back to the door and after a final glance outside, he slipped out of the cell, pushed the door closed behind him and left Nick alone.

Nick felt ill at ease that his cell mate had disappeared and the door had not been locked, anyone could come in. He got up, tried the handle and to his surprise found he could push the door open. He peered outside and saw inmates moving along the landing presumably down to tea. Just the thought of food made his stomach rumble but even though he was starving hungry he decided he would go without something to eat if it meant having to venture out on his own.

He gently pulled the door shut and sat back down on the chair. He had so much to learn; all the rules, how to avoid danger, where to find safety—if there was any. He looked round the cell wondering how many new inmates had sat in the same place worrying about the same sort of thing. He closed his eyes. This was the first day of his two year sentence—the thought threatened to overwhelm him.

The first night in prison is tough for anyone new to the system and it was no different for Nick Wood. It was still dark when he woke up on his first morning inside and at first he was confused and wondered where he was—but it didn't take long for him to remember. Even though he was knackered he propped himself up on one elbow and stared into the dark I might as well enjoy the silence while I can, he thought rubbing his eyes.

It had been the noise that had kept him awake for most of the night. He had longed for the safety of sleep and oblivion but the noise had been incredible. He couldn't believe how long the music had been allowed to go on for. Not that Nick minded loud music, he loved raves and the atmosphere that went with them, but neither Nick not Jason had a stereo to drown out the others. The torture had started at lights out and had carried on until way past two o'clock. Rave, jungle, heavy metal, even soul threatened to break down the walls of their cell.

Nick looked up at the mattress above his head. Jason hadn't been bothered by the noise. After returning to the cell he hadn't said a word, just ripped off his clothes, climbed up to his bunk and crashed out. By the sound of the snoring from above he was still asleep. Nick looked towards the sink in the corner and wondered if he dare get out of bed and get himself a drink of water. But he knew the tap made a racket and he didn't want to wake Jason. Despite the fact that the guy was thin and smaller than himself, he didn't want to antagonise him needlessly and get off on the wrong foot.

Daylight started to slowly filter in through the cell window and Nick guessed it was about six o'clock. He had about an hour to wait until the cell door opened. His stomach started rumbling again and he knew he would have to get something to eat at breakfast. He hoped Jason would go with him, but even if he didn't, he would still have to get food. He lay back and tried to think of something pleasant to while away the time, but nothing pleasant came to mind so he closed his eyes hoping that sleep would ease his worry.

* * *

At the same time as Nick was trying to get back to sleep, prison officer Les Wright was trying to keep awake as he drove to work. He was dog tired. It was only eight hours since his last shift, but the shortage of prison staff meant there was a lot of overtime going, which was useful to Les as he had promised to take his wife on a cruise the following year. Les was thinking about his holiday as he waited for the prison gate to open. Yes, he thought, two weeks somewhere warm away from this place.

He looked up at the rows of cell windows and reconciled himself with the fact that at least he wasn't locked away. On the second floor of 'C' wing Les spotted a figure standing at one of the cell windows. He worked out that it was Styles—better known to the prisoners as 'the Dragon' and he wondered why the man was up so early. Whatever the reason, he would be up to no good. With inmates like Styles on the landings there would always be trouble, especially for the young prisoners who couldn't protect themselves. Les thought back to his conversation with Tom the previous evening. He had told the lifer he would keep him informed about the new kid. Already Les had learned that Wood had been banged up with young Jason Smith—could be worse, he thought. But then again—according to rumours—could be better.

* * *

About an hour after Nick had unsuccessfully tried to get back to sleep, the lock on the cell door clicked open. Immediately Nick stuck his head out and called up to the top bunk. 'Are you awake Jason?' He had used the bucket for a pee during the night but he needed the loo now, his stomach was in knots. He called up to Jason again, hoping he was ready to get up and follow him to the washroom, but there was only silence from above and he knew he would have to venture out alone.

He got up, opened the cell door a couple of inches, peered outside and was relieved to find no-one there. He could see the washroom not more than ten yards away and he decided to take the chance. Quickly he slipped on his jeans and tee shirt, then in one hand he grabbed the toiletries he'd been given in reception. In the other he carried the slop bucket which was already beginning to smell like a public lavatory.

The washroom Nick entered was about the same size as the one they had at his old school. There were two sit down toilets but with only small partition doors there was hardly any privacy—anyone who was over six feet tall could easily see in. One of the toilets was occupied and Nick winced at the grunting noises coming from behind the closed door. The other cubicle appeared empty but to make sure he gently pushed on the door. With no-one shouting loudly at him he carried in the bucket and closed the door behind him. First he poured the slops away, careful not to splash the seat, then he sat down. All the time he was there he could hear inmates coming into the room and worried about leaving the safety of the loo. He probably took longer than he should have. Suddenly there was a loud thump on the door. 'Hurry up in there for fuck's sake—I need a shit,' came the voice.

Nick quickly pulled up his trousers and opened the door. The man looked closely at him as he came out. He was tall, stripped to the waist and had half his right ear missing. 'New in are you?' he asked. Nick was already feeling nervous and felt if he opened his mouth to reply he'd throw up on the man so he just nodded.

'Well don't take so fuckin' long next time,' the man said, pushing past him into the loo and shutting the door.

Nick glanced around the room to see if anyone was looking at him but fortunately all the inmates were busy. Spotting a vacant sink on the far side of the washroom he hurried across, filled it with water and started to wash himself with the prison soap he'd been given, realising it wasn't anything like the stuff his mum bought. This soap had bits in and felt like grade four sandpaper. While he literally scraped his hands and arms clean he could sense men around him, but not once did he look up. He also breathed through his mouth—the stench of the overnight slops being poured away made him want to retch. That morning he kept his eyes down, his mouth tightly shut, and got back to the cell as fast as he could, hoping Jason was awake and ready to go and get something to eat.

Nick had been pretty quick in the washroom, certainly a lot quicker than the time he took in the bathroom at home, and was surprised to find the cell empty when he returned. How the hell did Jason get out so fast he asked himself. For a moment he contemplated not bothering to go down for breakfast but he was so hungry he knew he had to make the effort. He quickly finished dressing, and after checking that the landing was clear he headed outside to experience his first meal in prison.

Down in the canteen Nick stood in line with a hundred other inmates waiting to collect his breakfast. In his hand he held the knife, fork and spoon he had collected from a trolley near the entrance of the canteen. At least I won't get stabbed with these he thought to himself as ran his thumb along the blunt edge of the knife.

In contrast to the darkness on the landings the canteen was glaringly lit and Nick felt as though he was sticking out like a sore thumb, the proverbial 'new boy.' I need someone to talk to, he decided. He could see Jason at the front of the queue but he was deep in conversation with other inmates and Nick didn't feel confident enough to join them, so he looked round to see if there was anyone else who looked remotely friendly, maybe someone his own age.

Only a few paces away there was a large black man leaning against the wall. Nick had never seen anyone so tall and thick set; his legs were huge and his neck must have been twice the size of Nick's. Not a guy I want to mix with, he thought. But Nick had let his gaze linger for too long and the man had caught him momentarily staring at him, his reaction was immediate. He heaved his bulk away from the wall and headed straight for Nick. 'What are you looking at boy?' he said.

'Nothing—honest,' blurted out Nick as he shrank back against the wall.

'You a sneaky grass?' asked the man threateningly.

Inwardly Nick screamed out the answer but he was so intimidated his defiant roar came out as a timid squeak. 'No,' he said lamely.

The brute raised his voice so that everyone nearby could hear. 'There's already one grass in this prison,' he said. The queue fell silent at the mention of the word. The man then leaned so close to Nick he could smell the stench of stale tobacco on his breath. 'If I find out it's you, you're a dead man,' he said poking Nick in the chest. For what seemed like ages the brute studied him like an insect, but the queue started to move and the man backed off.

Nick's breathing slowly returned to normal but he could feel beads of sweat prickling his forehead. Part of him just wanted to bolt back to the safety of his cell but instinctively he knew that would look suspicious and he had nothing to hide. He moved away from the wall and joined the end of the queue. He tried to look unconcerned as he waited, but he knew other inmates were now watching him. There'll be no more trying to make friends. That was it.

The queue inched forward at snail's pace, giving

Nick time to calm down and his hunger to return. Finally he reached the counter where the food was dished out. He'd waited a long time to get his first meal in prison, but he was soon to find out it wasn't much to wait for.

After visiting two counters Nick carried his tray across the canteen and studied his breakfast; some cold toast and a bowl of lumpy porridge. He thought back to when he was on bail and had heard a radio phone-in discussing prison life. He had found it reassuring to hear that everyone inside was having a cushy time in their luxury cells with an a la carte menu in the restaurants. He thought about the egg, bacon and sausage he presumed he'd be eating and then looked down at the food on his tray. He wished the people on the radio programme could be with him there that morning; feel the fear he felt when he was standing in the queue and then eat what was on his plate. They should talk about that on the radio, not how good it is inside, he thought.

Unclenching his jaw Nick looked around to see if he could find Jason but he was nowhere to be seen, so he wandered to a table with a couple of empty places. He didn't want to speak to the men already there but felt he just couldn't sit down. 'Okay if I sit here?' he asked. One of the men looked at him suspiciously then nodded. Nick climbed over the bench and placed his plate on the table. From his shirt pocket he took out the plastic knife, fork and spoon he'd collected, then stared at the gunge he was about to eat.

'What's up?' asked the man sitting opposite. 'Don't you want it?'

Nick hesitated not knowing what to say.

'Course he wants it,' came a voice from behind. 'Tuck in Nick, it's all you'll get till lunch.'

Jason plonked himself down, 'Not like the porridge mum makes, eh?' he said looking defiantly at the man opposite who slowly got up and moved off. Jason then placed four slices of toast and a large tin on the table. 'Help yourself to jam,' he said nodding to a filthy container which had dark congealed goo stuck to the sides.

'Thanks,' said Nick trying not to turn his nose up in disgust 'But erhm...

Jason grabbed the can and started to plaster the gunge onto his toast, 'You can't afford to be fussy—you'll starve. And another thing,' he said looking at Nick. 'You've gotta learn to stand up for yourself. You'll have everyone in the gaff comin' onto you for favours if you don't.'

Nick looked down absentmindedly at his porridge. Suddenly his mind was elsewhere. He was in prison because he hadn't stood up for himself. He knew he shouldn't have agreed to hand out the drugs the night of the rave and now he was paying the price. If only I'd been tough enough to say 'no'.

Nick felt a sharp kick on the shin. 'Eat up' said Jason. 'Stop daydreaming'.

It was enough to make Nick concentrate on the present and the porridge in front of him. 'I don't suppose you know where I could get some sugar?' he asked.

'You've gotta buy it—like everything else in 'ere,' said Jason at the same time as reaching into the top pocket of his shirt and taking out a small packet. ''Ere,' he said 'borrow some of mine.'

Nick took the sachet and making sure that no-one else saw, he poured some sugar on top of his porridge. He then neatly folded up the sachet and handed it back to Jason. 'Thanks,' he said, 'I owe you.'

'Too right you do,' said Jason.

With sugar helping to hide the taste it didn't take Nick long to swallow the lumps of porridge and eat his toast. While he was waiting for Jason to finish, he took the chance to look round the canteen. There were twelve long tables in the room and all were nearly full except one. It was in the far corner well away from the guards and Nick couldn't help but look closely at the men sitting down.

'What are you lookin' at?' asked Jason with urgency in his voice.

'The table over there,' said Nick nodding towards the far corner of the canteen. 'The one where the guys are smiling.' How could anyone be so at ease in a place like this? he wondered to himself. Nick noticed one man in particular. He was powerfully built—even bigger than Scarface. He had a shaved head and a tattoo on his neck around which hung a thick gold chain.

'Stop being so bleedin' obvious' said Jason. 'You shouldn't be lookin' over there.'

'Who are they?' asked Nick switching his gaze back to his own table. He was surprised to see the chain the man was wearing. He'd handed in the gold ring his mum had given him at reception for safe keeping and guessed this guy didn't have to worry about being mugged.

'They're guys you don't wanna meet,' said Jason. 'Mind your own business.'

Nick sat wondering who the men could be and it wasn't long before his curiosity got the better of him again. Out of the corner of his eye he glanced across the room and saw the men get up from the table and move towards the door. Just as the man with the gold chain was about to walk out he turned his head and looked straight back in Nick's direction. Nick could see him say something to the others and then they all looked round. Nick froze. Slowly he turned back to face Jason. They're talking about one of us, he thought and I hope it isn't me.

* * *

On the lifer's wing Tom shared breakfast with Shortie, his other next door neighbour. 'Did you 'ear about the trouble in the yard yesterday, Tom?'

'What was that then, Shortie?' Tom knew there had been a disturbance in the yard when an inmate had been stabbed with a knife made in the metal shop. One of them had had his cell searched by the guards for drugs and had thought the other bloke had grassed him up. When Shortie finished Tom sat back. Something nasty was happening inside Blackthorpe prison. There'd been more nickings for minor offences in the last few months than in the whole of the previous year; guys were being caught smoking the odd joint, cell searches were turning up illegal 'hooch', anything nicked out of the kitchens had been found immediately. Someone had to be passing notes to the governor and it was creating suspicion in every quarter.

'Not a healthy situation this 'grassing' business Shortie.'

'Remember when we had the same problem in Albany, Tom. We sorted it then all right.'

'Didn't we just,' said Tom, grimacing as he thought about the way they'd tracked down the grass and persuaded him to stop. 'Bit different now we're kept separate though,' he said referring to the fact that the lifers were now locked away on their own wing. 'At least it's not affecting us here yet.'

'I reckon it's got something to do with all the smack that's pouring into the prison,' said Shortie. 'While blokes are on the gear there'll always be trouble—always someone willing to sell their soul for a blind eye to be turned their way.'

Tom nodded—his friend was right. There was more smack in the prison than ever before. A few months after the governor had arrived at Blackthorpe he'd turned one of the older parts of the prison into a new 'drug free' wing and grouped the addicts together in one place. On paper Tom knew it would make the governor look as though he was trying to control the drug problem, but the wing had turned into a nightmare. The special drug course he'd promised had never materialised and there was more 'smack' there now than in the rest of the prison put together.

Shortie dragged Tom's mind back from the hell of the smack 'eads wing to the problems they might soon face. 'What happens if it does start to affect us?' he asked

'Might have to be action stations again,' said Tom.

Chapter 3

'Wood, over here!' shouted a guard as Nick was making his way back to his cell after breakfast with Jason. Nick walked over to the short stocky man as Jason carried on upstairs. 'Need you to sign a form,' the guard said walking into his office. Nick followed and watched the guard pick up a folder and take out a piece of paper. He put it on the table and held out a pen.

'What am I signing Guv?' he asked.

'You're signing for this,' he said holding up a special card that could be used to make calls on the prison phones. 'We let all new prisoners have one so they can tell their families where they are, but it's the only one you'll get free.'

Nick signed the form and took the phone card. 'Thanks, Guv,' he said.

'I'd put it in your pocket if I was you, there are

blokes in here that would kill for one of those.' Nick looked at the card, decided to take the guards advice and slipped it in his trouser pocket.

'Don't forget you've got induction at ten o'clock,' the guard said.

'Yes, Guv,' said Nick not daring to ask what induction was all about. He walked out of the office and then bounded up the stairs taking two-at-a-time intent on catching up with Jason. But at the top of the second flight he came to an abrupt stop as a big guy with long black greasy hair stepped out from the shadows and blocked his way. Nick recognised him immediately as one of the men he had watched leaving the canteen.

'What's the hurry kid—got somewhere to go?'

There was a movement behind him and instinctively Nick knew that someone was now blocking his retreat. He tried to control his breathing telling himself not to panic.

'What've you been up to?' asked the brute. 'Got a little present from the screws 'ave you?'

'No,' replied Nick staring back defiantly and hoping that he looked braver than he felt. From behind a pair of hands clamped themselves onto his shoulders and he was pushed roughly towards the stair railings. Within seconds he was bent over the top rail with his top half dangling in mid air.

'You wanna take your time. Accidents 'appen when you run. You could've taken a nasty fall,' Nick was pushed further over the rail and he could feel hands rummaging through his pockets. Blood rushed to his head and he felt faint as he stared through the safety net to the floor below.

The man holding him from behind grabbed Nick by the hair and yanked his head back. 'Where is it?' he said roughly. Suddenly a voice boomed up the stairwell. 'What's going on up there?'

'Tell 'im nothing or I'll plunge you,' said the man pulling a short, sharp blade from his pocket and holding it threateningly against Nick's neck.

Nick didn't hesitate. 'Nothing Guv,' he called down.

The thug at his side took a step back away from the railing so he couldn't be seen but the man behind put his lips to Nick's ear. 'There won't always be a guard around to save you,' he whispered.

Then as quickly as they appeared the men were gone. Nick looked round carefully making sure no-one else was there to attack him, but the landing was empty. The adrenaline rush he'd experienced from hanging over the rail, a primeval coping mechanism, started to lessen and his legs suddenly felt weak and his hands started to tremble. He gripped the rail to steady himself and as quickly as possible made his way back to the relative safety of his cell.

Jason could tell something was wrong as soon his cell mate walked through the door, 'Jesus! You're as white as a sheet.'

Nick told Jason what had happened. 'I thought they were going to push me over the rail or stab me,' he said.

'Sounds like the Dragon's bully boys.'

'The Dragon?'

'Yeah—the bald headed bloke you asked about in the canteen—he's got a tattoo of a dragon on his neck.'

'I caught him staring at me,' Nick said.

'That's it then. He set his boys on you. They'll duff you up just enough to scare you, then 'Enter the Dragon'. He'll be your saviour—for a price.'

'But I haven't got anything to give him,' said Nick. Then he suddenly thought about the phone card. 'I think they were after this,' he said taking it out of his pocket and showing it to Jason.

Jason smirked. 'That and more besides,' he said.

'What do you mean?'

'His protection doesn't come cheap, he'll want more than one phone card. You'll have to find something more to give 'im or your life won't be worth living.'

Jason then leaned across with a serious expression on his face and grabbed Nick by the arm. 'Listen Nick, there are three golden rules to surviving in prison. I'm guilty of breaking all three, to my cost. So it's a case of do as I say, not as I do. Rule one— don't lend. Rule two—don't borrow. Rule three—don't do no-one no favours. Now because I'm an idiot, I'm going to break two of them rules. I'm goin' to do you a favour and offer you a piece of free advice . Whenever you see the Dragon heading your way turn tail and run. Get out of there fast. Doesn't matter where you are or what you're doing.'

Nick swallowed hard, 'I couldn't have avoided what happened just now.'

Jason shook his head, 'You've gotta have your wits about you all the time.'

'All the time? You mean you're never able to walk anywhere without the fear of getting set on?'

'Too right, you need eyes in the back of your head in 'ere.'

Nick sat down and rested his head on the table. How can anyone survive in here? he asked himself. Not for the first time and it wouldn't be the last he regretted the night when he took a risk and had sentenced himself to prison hell.

Jason sat back and rolled himself a large cigarette. ''Ere, I'll break another rule,' he said. 'Gonna give you something to make you feel better.'

'What's that?' Nick asked, looking up.

'Try one of these.'

Nick watched Jason light up the huge roll-up and realised it was a joint. 'What if a screw comes in, he'll smell it.'

'We can 'ear their fairy feet a mile away. Chill out Nick. Do yourself a favour and get stoned.' Jason took a drag then exhaled into Nick's face. Nick breathed in the smoke. Just a few drags and his troubles would be gone and for a while the nightmare would be over. 'Take it,' said Jason holding out the joint. Nick hesitated. 'Go on,' goaded Jason. 'Or do you wanna do your bird the hard way?'

Nick held out his hand, telling himself he could easily say 'no', but he didn't want to.

* * *

Tom Hawks nailed the picture to the wall and stood back to study his latest attempt at painting. Not bad he thought to himself. Then he smiled. Not all that good, either. Tom recognised his limitations. He would never be a brilliant artist but, what the hell, it helped pass the time. He heard someone come into the cell but he didn't turn round. 'Nice painting, Tom.'

'Hi Les, what can I do for you?' asked Tom recognising the voice.

'I'm keeping out of the way,' said the guard venturing further into the cell.

'Oh, yeah, what's going on now?'

'All hell's about to break loose on 'B' Wing,' said Les, sitting down on the only chair. Tom sat down on his bed and took out his tobacco pouch. "What's brewing?"

Les shook his head. 'That's just it—not a lot. The governor's been informed there's hooch stashed in the broom cupboard and he's on his way down there now. You know how he likes to show off. I reckon even you lifers will be banged up this weekend.'

'If we get banged up, Les, it becomes personal. They can do what they want out there, but when it affects us, the rules change. The grass will have to be dealt with.'

'We hate it just as much as you Tom. We want a quiet life on the wings, you know that.' he said. 'Have you got any idea who it could be Tom?

'No idea, none at all.' said Tom shaking his head. Even if he did know he wouldn't tell a screw, not even Les. The boys dealt with that kind of thing in their own way.

* * *

Just before ten o'clock Nick sat in the induction room on his own wondering where everyone was. The joint he had smoked had taken effect. His head swam and he felt tired. For ten minutes he sat and lounged in the chair before it dawned on him that perhaps he was in the wrong place. Then two of the prisoners he had travelled with in the van sauntered in. Five minutes after that Scarface turned up followed by an officer carrying a clip board.

'Right you lot,' said the officer who stood before them. 'One of you hasn't been in prison before so I'd better explain what's meant to happen.' He looked at Nick who immediately felt uncomfortable.

'Whilst you're in prison you're meant to be rehabilitated so you don't commit the crimes again. That's meant to involve education and courses to find out why you committed the crimes in the first place. But the prison hasn't got that kind of funding so you lot work instead.'

The officer continued in a cold clinical voice. 'Most first-timers come in with good intentions,' he said looking directly at Nick. 'But either the hooch, the drugs, or the system gets them. When they eventually get out, if they're still in one piece, they won't be able to get a job 'cos no-one wants to employ anyone with a criminal record. But they need money to pay the bills, and the only way to get it is to steal it. So they end up back in here. It's a vicious circle that's very difficult to break.'

Nick tried not to let the guard's depressing talk get him down. No matter how hard it would be, when he was released, he was determined not to get into trouble again.

For the next half an hour the officer told them about the prison and the work they would be expected to do. Apart from the occasional lecture on health and safety, they would have to stay in their cells for the rest of the week. Work would start after the weekend and, for their forty hours a week, they would each be paid approximately seven pounds. Out of that money they were expected to buy all toiletries, their phone cards and any luxuries like tobacco and food.

After running through the prison rules, the officer told them about the other activities that were available in the prison. There was a library, a gym, a woodwork room and an art and craft section. At the mention of the art section Nick focused his attention on what the officer was saying but his flicker of interest was quickly extinguished by the officer.

'Don't get too excited, Wood. The art room's small and there's a long waiting list. If you want to put your name down you'd best go to see the head of art this afternoon, but don't expect much, you're going to work everyday.'

At the end of the meeting the officer gave each one of the prisoners a sheet of writing paper and a pen and said that if they wanted to write home instead of phoning, the prison would pay for one letter. He also explained that each new inmate was entitled to a 'reception' visit and that they should notify their prospective visitors in the letter. Then they were dismissed.

Back in his cell Nick sat on the far side of the small table. He was still unnerved that the cell door wasn't locked and felt safer facing the door rather than having his back to it. He sat with his elbows resting on the table trying to work out how to get in touch with home. He didn't want to talk to his mum on the phone, as he wasn't sure if she'd have a go at him and he'd decided to try and write. He stared at the blank sheet of paper in front of him, fiddled with his pen and wondered what to say. It wouldn't be enough to tell his mum he was sorry for the trouble he'd caused. He groaned inwardly as he recalled how many times his mother had warned him about getting involved with the rich kids. 'How can you keep up with them?' she'd asked when he'd told her that one of his new friends was the son of an Earl, and that his girlfriend's dad had a house in the country, a flat in London and a villa in the Bahamas.

'I can handle it, mum,' he'd said. 'They like me, they know the score, they know I'm broke—it's not a problem.'

His mother had shaken her head, 'You can't keep up with people like that,' she'd warned. And he had laughed. 'I think you're an inverted snob, mum,' he'd said.

He had insisted that if she knew them she would change her mind. And when Jessica had offered to give him a lift home at the end of the summer term last year, he'd been glad of the opportunity to show her off to his mum. 'Don't get the wrong idea mum, Jessica and me. We're only friends nothing more.' The meeting had seemed to go down well with both his mum and his girlfriend. Jessica had declined his mum's invitation to stay the night, she was flying out to Jamaica the next day.

After Jessica roared away in her VW Cabriolet, he'd gone back into the kitchen and confronted his mum. 'Well?' he said. 'What did you think?' His mum had shrugged, 'Don't come crying to me when things go wrong.'

Nick threw down the pen, stood up and paced the cell. He wanted to write and tell his mum that he was looking forward to her visiting. But would it be fair to ask her to come and visit this place? Hadn't she been through enough? He sat down again and picked up the pen. Perhaps she might be thinking the same thing. She might not want to visit me in prison, he thought, and I wouldn't blame her if she didn't.

Looking for inspiration he bent down, reached underneath his bunk and pulled out the small bag of personal possessions he had been allowed to keep and took out the photo of his mum and sister and put them on the table. They both looked so happy. He'd taken the picture on a day out to Brighton, just the three of them. He sat and stared at the picture, letting his mind think back to the good times. Eventually he picked up the pen and started to write. At first he found it difficult to know what to say, but soon words started to flow across the page. Nick didn't expect them to forget the pain he'd caused, but he hoped one day they might forgive him. He knew the neighbours would already be pointing fingers and talking behind their backs. In many respects their lives would be even harder than his own, but even if his mum didn't forgive him, she had to be worried about him and in the letter he tried hard not to make prison sound too bad. He said he was coping well and glossed over what prison was really like. He certainly didn't want to let her know how filthy and dangerous the place was.

At the end of the letter, almost hidden away for fear of the invitation being turned down, he said that if she and his sister wanted to, they could visit him and he hoped they would. In a way the fear of being rejected by his family was even worse than having to deal with the Dragon.

Just as he was reading through his letter, the

door of the cell burst open and two men came rushing in. Nick reacted as fast as he could but he wasn't nearly fast enough. He had been concentrating on his letter and barely had time to glance up. Before he knew it, he was grabbed, spun round and flung across the bottom bunk and pinned to the bed with a knee in his back.

'We've come for a little chat,' came a low, gravely voice. Nick's head was pressed so hard into the mattress he started to choke. Struggling like an eel he managed to swivel his head slightly to the right and was just about to shout out for help when a hand clamped itself firmly over his mouth. He tried to see his attackers out of the corner of his eye but all he could see was a dragon on the man's neck.

Chapter 4

Nick was totally overpowered. Once he stopped wrestling the man took his hand away from his mouth, the pressure on his back eased and Nick was able to turn round to face his attackers. A gold chain dangled in front of his face.

'Know who I am?' asked the Dragon.

Nick shook his head. 'No,' he said, not daring to admit that he did.

'They call me the Dragon—on account of this.' He pointed to his neck and the tattoo. 'Good eh?' he said proudly.

Nick stared at the tattoo. You'd have to be a psycho to have that thing stuck on your neck, he thought. He wanted to say that the drawing was naff and that given five minutes he could do better, but he kept his mouth firmly shut. 'That's right, take a good look. I want you to see it in your sleep.'

The man standing next to the Dragon reached down and gripped the top of Nick's with fingers that felt like steel and hauled him to his feet. He was a small man with a narrow long nose and eyes set too close together. He looked like a weasel and his fingers felt like claws. 'Rough place prison,' he sneered. 'Someone like you needs protection.'

'We deal in protection, amongst other things,' said the Dragon breaking into a smile. 'A little birdie tells me that you've done a bit of drug dealing yourself.'

Nick shook his head. 'No,' he said. 'It was only the once.'

'Glad to hear it. You'd better keep it that way. This is my patch. Understand?'

Nick nodded. 'Whatever you say.'

'There's a good lad,' said the weasel, patting him roughly on the head.

The Dragon took a tobacco pouch out of his pocket, picked out a ready rolled cigarette and lit up. Nick immediately recognised the smell. The Dragon held out the joint ''Ere, for you.'

'No thanks,' said Nick. 'I don't do drugs.'

The Dragon laughed. 'We've heard that before,' he said. 'You'll find it tough doin' bird without a bit of help.'

Nick tried to look defiant but for his pains he received a sharp slap in the face and the force spun him back against the table. The Weasel took a pace towards him with his fist raised to deliver a harder blow and instinctively Nick put his arm up to shield himself. The Dragon stepped in and held back the Weasel's arm.

'Now as for protection, that's another matter,' said the Dragon. 'Pay me every week and I'll make sure that no-one takes advantage of you.'

'But I haven't got any money,' Nick blurted out. He was all choked up. Although he spoke the words it sounded like someone else's voice.

'Aah,' said the Dragon. 'You're making my heart bleed. Just to show you I'm a reasonable man you can keep the phone card you got this morning and I'll give you a week before I expect the first payment—four quid,'

'But I might not be able to get that much,' complained Nick.

'Four quid's the going rate kid.'

'But...'

The reaction was immediate and proved to be the lesson the Dragon had turned up to give. The punch came from nowhere and thundered into Nick's ribs. He doubled over with pain and gasped for breath. Still winded the Dragon grabbed him by the hair, pulled his head back and stuck his face so close his gold chain brushed against Nick's chin. 'We take the money in phone cards,' he said menacingly. 'We collect Friday night straight after canteen. Don't be late or it'll be double the following week. Miss that and we'll cut that pretty face of yours.'

The Dragon let go of Nick's hair and pushed him back against the bed. He then signalled to the Weasel that it was time to go. On his way out the Weasel flashed out his foot in a vicious kick and the toe of his steel-capped boot caught Nick square on the thigh. Nick crumpled to the floor in agony. He stayed there not daring to move until he heard the footsteps outside disappear. Tears filled his eyes, and he was shaking uncontrollably. Gingerly he pulled himself up onto his bunk and curled himself up into a ball. His ribs hurt so much his breaths were short and shallow. It felt as if his leg was broken. Nick's body had never taken blows like this before and he cringed with fear at the thought that it might happen again—but next time even worse. Curled up on his bed all he could think about were knives and scars.

When Jason returned for lunch the smell of dope hit him as soon as he walked through the door. 'What's all this then, another spliff, where did you get it?' he asked, laughing.

Nick hadn't moved for an hour but when Jason came into the cell he had eased himself round. He looked towards his cell mate. 'It wasn't mine,' he said.

From the sound of Nick's voice Jason could tell that something wasn't right. He looked more closely at his cell mate on the bottom bunk and could now see that Nick was in pain. Slowly the light dawned. 'The Dragon's been to visit,' he surmised. With a resigned sigh he sat down on a chair and took out his tobacco. 'How much did he ask for?'

'Four quid a week. Said he'd cut me if I don't get it. It'll leave me with hardly anything even if I get my full wage.'

'Tell me about it,' said Jason.

'But how does everyone cope?' asked Nick.

'There are ways to get a bit of extra cash,' he said. "Some guys make jewellery boxes in the wood work room and sell 'em to the visitors. That's a nice little earner—try that.'

Nick was still lying down but with the possibility of a solution to his problem he propped himself up onto one elbow and focused his attention more closely on what his cell mate was saying. But wood work wasn't the answer. 'I've always been useless at wood work. No-one in their right mind would buy a box I made,' he said.

'You must be good at something?'

'I can paint,' he said.

'What—paint and decorate? I can't see you being allowed to do anything that useful.'

'No, I mean paint pictures, I've always been good at art. That's what I did at college.'

'That's your answer then. Some of the work the art class does gets sold in the visits hall for about four quid. Get down the art department.'

'But I've been told there's a waiting list—I won't get a place.'

Jason looked at him with a withering expression, 'Don't listen to that crap. Go sell yourself,' he said. 'Tell 'em they've got a budding Picasso on their hands.'

'Hardly,' said Nick. But he lay back wondering if the idea might work. He'd always been talented at art. At school he'd been told if he worked hard he might even make a living at it. But at college he'd just done the bare minimum to get by; all he'd been interested in was impressing his rich friends. He didn't know that one day his life might depend on his ability to paint. As he lay on the bed he regretted not listening more closely to his tutors and wondered if he was good enough at art to sell any pictures. He held up his right hand and looked at it closely. Maybe his safety literally lay in his hands.

* * *

That afternoon, when all the inmates had gone to work and the Dragon was nowhere to be seen, Nick hobbled downstairs and handed in his open letter to the guards. He'd been told at induction that nothing was allowed out of the prison before being thoroughly checked. It was tight security; all telephone calls were recorded, all letters read. Only when the guard had finished inspecting the contents of the letter and envelope, was he allowed to post it in the red box attached to the wall outside the guard's office.

Jason had told Nick that every wing had a similar box and not only was it the place where letters home were posted. All formal complaints to the governor, about the lousy food, the lack of exercise and the intolerable noise went through this channel. The screws used them as an excuse not to listen to an inmate sounding off, 'Post it in the box,' they would say. But the inmates knew that notes to the governor would rarely be acted upon, unless it was from a grass. It was suspected that it was this way the grass in Blackthorpe was getting information to the governor. It was the most efficient method of informing on another inmate with the least chance of getting caught.

After posting his letter and explaining to the guards where he was going, Nick wandered through the prison towards the education department. A day earlier he would have been apprehensive about moving through the prison on his own, but he was now driven by his sense of survival. He was heading towards the middle of the prison near the medical centre and the nearer he got to the education department, the fewer inmates became visible. Nick knew that most were at work, but he expected to see at least some. It was eerie walking along the corridors with hardly anyone around.

When he finally reached the art and craft section, hobbling all the way on his painful leg, he peered through the windows of some of the classrooms. They reminded him of the ones in his old school but here there was no noise and mayhem. In fact there was very little here at all; a few old computers covered in dust in one room; a pottery room that was deserted; just a handful of prisoners doing some carpentry in another. It felt to Nick as if he was walking through a ghost town. Finally he found the room he had been looking for and for a moment he waited outside, thinking over what he wanted to say.

Amy Jones sat in the art room busy sorting through her students' artistic attempts. She was hoping that at least one of the paintings might be good enough to be put on display in the visiting hall. She smiled at some of the strange efforts. Someone had painted a picture of her although it looked more like an alien out of Star Trek. Perhaps she could exhibit it and use that as the title. However, the lack of talent didn't make her feel despondent. She enjoyed teaching the inmates and she knew they appreciated her. It felt good to be able to help add colour to their grey, drab lives.

More importantly she felt that some of her students used painting as a therapy, temporarily helping them to forget where they were. She glanced up at the clock above the door and saw someone hovering outside. Through the opaque glass she only could see that the person was short and of small frame. 'Come in,' she called at the same time as realising that she was alone. Tom Hawks the lifer had warned her not to be so trusting and as the door opened she glanced down at the emergency button under her desk.

When she saw the young man who entered, she quickly decided he posed no threat. Her first thought was that he looked no older than her son. But he was only eighteen. What was this place coming to? she asked herself as she studied the scrawny young man who stood in front of her shuffling from foot to foot, obviously too nervous to speak. 'What can I do for you?' she asked.

It was a nice surprise for Nick to see a woman working in Blackthorpe. He'd heard there were a couple of women officers in the prison but they weren't on his wing.

'I've come to see about enrolling for the art class Miss,' he said to the woman who looked about the same age as his mum. Her dark hair was tied on top of her head and she wore a clean pair of navy blue overalls.

'Have you now?' the woman said. 'Take a seat.

My name's Any Jones. And you are?'

'Wood 582 Miss.'

The education staff had been told not to become too familiar with the inmates and there was no need to ask the next question, but she was an art teacher in prison for a reason. She could have applied for a better paid job at the local college but against all the protests from her family she had accepted the job in the prison. Everyone who knew her thought she was crazy but it had proved to be the most rewarding job she had undertaken. And no matter what the prison officers told her, she tried to show kindness to new inmates. She gave the boy a reassuring smile. 'I mean your first name,' she said.

The simple question was so unexpected it tore right through Nick's defences. The episode with the Dragon had left him feeling vulnerable and alone but he'd managed to keep control in front of Jason. Suddenly a simple demonstration of kindness from someone he'd never seen before had torn down his brave facade. He looked away, tears welling up in his eyes and he pinched himself hard in the back of the hand. An embarrassing silence enveloped the room as he tried to regain some control but when he turned back to answer his bottom lip was trembling. 'Nick,' he said quietly.

Amy could see that Nick was struggling with his emotions and to give him a few seconds she leant forward and wrote his name down on a sheet of paper on her desk. She felt sorry for Nick Wood, but then again she felt sorry for most of the inmates she came into contact with. But sympathy was the last thing this boy needed if he was to survive his time in Blackthorpe.

'Is there a particular reason why you want to enrol on the course?' she asked in a more official voice without looking up.

John Hoskison

Nick could taste blood in his mouth where he'd bitten his lip. Those few seconds had been enough for him to regain control and he knew he had to create a good impression. He pulled himself up to his full height. 'Yes Miss, I need to earn some extra money—I was told that students can sell their paintings.'

Amy raised an eyebrow. 'You'll need a better reason than that, I can only take ten students at a time, and it's popular.'

Nick could hear the negative tone in her reply. 'I used to be an art student,' he said trying to convince her to give him a chance. 'I need to paint, it's my life.' Nick felt it might not be too far from the truth.

The young man was obviously trying his hardest to impress her but she was rather cynical about his claim to have studied art, she'd heard that too many times before and earning extra money by selling paintings was not the primary goal of her art department. However, there was no harm in giving Nick Wood an opportunity to prove himself.

'I'll put your name down, but, you'll have to wait your turn. There won't be a place for at least a month.' she said.

Nick let out an audible groan. A vision of being beaten to pulp with his face slashed badly flashed through his mind. 'That's no good Miss—I need to start straight away.'

Alarm bells rang in Amy's mind. 'The money isn't for drugs is it?' she asked suspiciously.

Nick shook his head, 'No Miss I don't touch drugs,' he said discounting the spliff he had smoked with Jason as a one off.

Amy Jones sat back in her chair trying to decide what to do. It was in her power to help the boy but she'd heard such denials before only to find out she'd been deceived. But she had to admit that this young man seemed different. Maybe he needed money

48

for something other than drugs, after all, she didn't understand everything that happened on the wings and if he was an art student it would be good for the department and good for him.

'I can't put you on the course but I can give you a few paint pots and paper,' she said. 'You can take them back to your cell, paint in your spare time and if your work is any good, I'll see what I can do about putting it on sale in the visits room.'

Nick breathed a sigh of relief. He knew this was the best he was going to get and it was a lifeline that might save him. 'That would be great Miss,' he said enthusiastically.

Amy got up and went to one of the cupboards. She was taking a risk trusting Nick Wood but the equipment she was giving him was old and even if she never saw him again, it wouldn't hurt the department. For a while she rummaged through the shelves and eventually took out a small box and two rolls of paper which she handed over to Nick.

'Thanks Miss,' he said looking at the equipment he had just been given. 'I'll paint over the weekend and bring the picture in Monday if that's okay?'

'That'll be fine,' she answered hoping the young man's obvious enthusiasm would last that long. Nick smiled, turned round and hobbled towards the door. From behind Amy called out. 'Nick, what happened to your leg?'

'Oh, nothing Miss,' he said continuing on his way but trying not to hobble quite so much. He was far too embarrassed to tell her he'd been beaten up.

Chapter 5

Back in his cell Nick put down the rolled paper and box of paints on the table. Inside the box he found two brushes. One obviously for fine detail, the other for bold thick strokes. He picked up the brushes to inspect them. They were old and tatty and he couldn't help think about the brilliant equipment that had been available to him at college. Not that he'd ever used it, he'd spent all his spare time partying. Mentally he pinched himself, he had to concentrate on the job in hand. Thinking about lost opportunities was going to get him no where.

He held the brushes up to the light and scrutinised them. Several times in the past, when he had been at school and painting regularly, he had completed pictures only to find small hairs spoiling the overall effect. He plucked a few loose ones from the brushes he had been given before he was satisfied, then he looked closely at the paper. He recalled his old art master droning on and on about the quality of paper and how it could effect the ability to alter colours. If it's too smooth the paint can take ages to dry. Changing shades can be quite easy in those circumstances. This paper was porous however and Nick knew that he would have to get the colours correct before applying them.

It took several minutes for Nick to finish preparing all the materials, but at the end he still hadn't decided what to paint. It had to be simple because he wanted to show it to Amy Jones at the first opportunity, to get some money in as quickly as possible.

Nick looked round his drab cell for inspiration. The walls were filthy, the floor was cold concrete and the window had a crack in it from top to bottom. There was no colour in prison and there was nothing there to inspire him. He sat down heavily in the chair. Studying the cell in such a clinical way had brought it home to him where he was and what he was missing. For the first time in prison he longed for freedom and wide open spaces. In the past he had never appreciated the fields round the back of his house, but now he would have given anything to smell the grass and breathe in the fresh air. Suddenly he knew what he was going to paint. Locked away behind the walls of the most colourless place he had ever seen, the magnificent fields at the back of his house seemed more than appropriate.

Nick sat down, breathed in deeply and picked up the thicker of the two brushes.

He closed his eyes and concentrated. Deeper and deeper he went until at last his imagination let him escape beyond the prison walls. For several minutes he sat and stared at the scene he had created in his mind and then finally he opened his eyes. Absentmindedly he mixed the necessary colours and then, as if in a trance, he started to paint. For the first time since entering prison, Nick Wood forgot his troubles and became lost in his own imaginary world.

* * *

Prisoner 582 wasn't the only person feeling at one with himself that afternoon. The governor of Blackthorpe sat in his office looking at the letter he had just received from the Home Office, the government department responsible for all prisons. It contained results from the latest survey on prison efficiency. He smiled and congratulated himself on Blackthorpe's excellent record. Up twenty percent for illegal alcohol convictions. Up fifteen percent on convictions of theft. Up eighteen percent on convictions for possessing drugs, and there was a special congratulatory note about the introduction of a 'drug free' wing. Yes—it made very good reading.

He thought back to the deal he had made with one of the prisoners that was partly responsible for the success. The other prisoners would no doubt call him a grass, but the inmate was very useful to the governor. The regular notes he was passed were responsible for the high conviction rate in the prison. Okay, so it was a pain having to look after the grass, making sure he got a good job, that sort of thing, but overall it was clearly worth his while. Some might argue that the prison was becoming a very unhappy place, but what did the prisoners expect, a holiday camp? The governor was gaining a good reputation, he operated well within his budget, yet he still produced outstanding results.

He sat back in his comfy leather chair and congratulated himself again. Being informed about the hooch on 'B' wing was an excellent break. Just when it looked as though he would have to part with even more overtime wages, he now had a good excuse to bang up the inmates for the weekend and let the guards go home. From out of his desk drawer he took out a piece of paper and started writing a memo to the senior officer. This deal with the grass is working out just fine, he thought to himself.

* * *

Nick was painting at his desk when the door to his cell swung open. He froze mid stroke but was relieved to see it was only Jason returning from his day's work.

'Blimey, you're twitchy,' Jason said pushing the door shut behind him and moving across to the table. He picked up one of the brushes Nick had been using. 'Christ, where did you nick this from?' he asked.

'I didn't nick it, it was given to me.'

Jason looked at Nick's picture. 'You haven't done much,' he said.

'It takes time to get things right,' Nick said defensively, looking at the background he had nearly completed. Jason looked unimpressed. He picked up the paint box, licked his finger and wiped it across one of the sections. The end of his finger turned a bright red which he looked at with interest before wiping it clean on his overalls. 'You should paint something with blood and guts in it,' he said. 'You'll see enough in 'ere.' The remark was meant to be a joke but Nick swallowed at the thought. Jason climbed up to his bunk bed and lay down. 'How was induction?' he asked.

'Boring,' Nick said wiping his brushes and packing away his equipment. 'They told us about the different work here, that's all really.'

'Did they tell you where you'll be placed?'

'Not yet, said they'd let us know tomorrow.'

'In the laundry I'd guess. Tell 'em you're good at folding sheets, you'll be put in with me,' said Jason.

Nick thought of his mum and how she'd given up trying to get him to fold anything. 'I'll give it a try,' he said, not holding out much hope.

'I wouldn't be able to survive without the laundry,' said Jason. 'That's how I earn the extra money I need to pay off the Dragon.'

'How?' asked Nick.

'I do his washing for 'im. He lets me off some of the dosh I owe.'

'You have to pay four quid a week as well?' asked Nick, astonished that someone so streetwise would be in the same position as himself.

A laugh erupted from the top bunk. 'Wish it was,' said Jason. 'But I'm into him for a bit more than that.'

'How come?' asked Nick. Jason peered down at him from the top bunk. 'I'm on the gear,' he said.

'What? Heroin!'

'That's what I'm in 'ere for really,' he said. 'I've 'ad to nick stuff to pay for me habit. Problem is when I'm banged up I try to come off the gear but there's more smack in 'ere than on the outside.'

Nick had mixed with people who took a few 'E"s in the past, and there were always one or two at college who smoked the odd joint, but only one student was reputed to have taken heroin. It was meant to be the worst. Smack'eads are violent nutters,' he'd been told. He looked up to the top bunk. 'Isn't it dangerous?' he asked.

'It's nothing I can't handle,' said Jason.

Chapter 6

Life in the outside world continued as normal that weekend, but a depression settled over Blackthorpe prison during the enforced 'bang up'. The governor had issued instructions for the prison to be shut down for the weekend, while it was searched. Friday night saw the only signs of rebellion, but with everyone locked behind doors, Saturday and Sunday passed without incident. Had the prison been a living entity, it's metabolism and heartbeat would have slowed to almost zero.

Nick woke up before the cell door opened on Monday morning. He was becoming good at guessing the time by the amount of daylight in the cell and guessed there was still half an hour to go. Normally some signs of life could be heard by then and the silence was eerie. He lay back and thought about the events of the last three days. The panic had started on Friday when the notice from the governor was posted outside the canteen. Nick had seen it first as he was standing at the back of the food queue waiting to collect his food. 'What does it say?' asked Jason who was talking to another prisoner on the other side of the corridor.

'Hooch was found on 'B' wing and the governor wants the prison searched. We're all to be banged up for the weekend.'

'What, the whole fuckin' time?' gasped Jason. Nick's cell mate hadn't been the only one shocked by the news. All over the prison inmates started running round like headless chickens, panicking at the thought of being confined to their cells for forty eight hours.

'I've gotta get something that'll help me through the two days,' Jason had said over lunch.

'What—like a good book?' asked Nick.

Jason had laughed. 'Something a bit better than that,' he said. 'I don't read books. There's only one thing that'll help me pass the time.'

Nick knew what he meant and his heart had sunk at the thought of being locked up for the weekend with someone high on heroin.

Just as he suspected Jason had come staggering back to the cell on Friday night smiling and as high as a kite. Music from another cell blasted out, and when the door closed Jason had leapt onto the table imitating Johnny Rotten of The Sex Pistols singing 'I am the anti Christ.' An hour later he was still going strong when the 'bang up' protest started.

It began with one inmate kicking his door in frustration, shouting at the top of his voice. Then someone else had joined in, the same way it had started in the prison van. Before long the whole wing was at it—Jason had loved it. He'd put on his heavy work boots and with his back to the door had lashed out like a bucking bronco Bang! Bang! Bang! The noise was earth shattering, enough to wake the dead, but not enough to disturb the duty guards. They didn't re-act. They'd seen it all before. They knew the heavy steel doors could withstand the onslaught and simply waited for the anger and frustration to subside. It was then that Jason crashed out on his bunk where he remained for most of the weekend. Even when they had been allowed out to collect their meals and throw out their slops, Jason had remained asleep on his bed. Thankfully, Nick's worst fears of what it would be like to be banged up with someone high on heroin had not been realised. Perhaps it's all a myth, he thought. Jason hadn't seemed so bad.

Nick sat up and massaged his neck, which was stiff from painting for hours on end. Thankfully he had found his own way of escaping the depression of the enforced bang up. He looked across the room to where he'd left his picture to dry underneath the table near the hot pipe. Without making any noise Nick crept out of bed. Carefully he picked up the painting and studied it. The first signs of morning light were starting to illuminate the cell and although he couldn't see the contrast of colours, he could see the overall form of the painting. He was pleased, but he wasn't the judge. He just hoped that Amy Jones would think it worth putting on display.

Suddenly the door clicked open showing it was seven o'clock. He looked up to the top bunk to see if Jason was awake, but his friend hadn't moved.

'Hey Jason wake up,' he said 'It's time to get up.' He tried again but Jason just moaned and turned round to face the wall. Giving up, Nick carefully replaced his picture and started to get ready. Just before lights out on Friday he'd been told to report to the laundry first thing Monday morning. The guard had issued him with some working overalls and a pair of heavy looking boots. He wished Jason was ready to go with him, but after having a last look at his cell mate he decided he wouldn't be going anywhere at all.

Not in that state, thought Nick. Not wanting to be late, he slipped on his new overalls, stuffed his feet into his boots and headed out to prepare for his first morning at work. He left the slop bucket for Jason to empty. It was his turn.

* * *

Tom Hawks sat next to Shortie in the lifer's canteen and toyed with his porridge. Normally he wolfed it down but his mind was on other things. And that was the problem. The art of surviving twenty-odd years in prison was to do as little thinking as possible. Every day would then seem like another, the seasons would become a blur and the years would tick by while you were on auto pilot. But having to think, brought one back into the real world, where time dragged. Somehow he had slogged his way through the forty eight hours of enforced bang up, but he'd hated every minute. It wasn't as though he, or any of the other lifers, had done anything wrong.

When would the governor get it through his head that the lifers only want peace and quiet, he thought to himself, while grinding his spoon into the bottom of his bowl. For the first time in ages Tom longed to be back in the real world where he could rejoin the human race.

Shortie could sense his friend was disturbed. 'It's the grass that's causing the problem Tom,' he said shaking his head. 'Without all the info the grass is passing on, this nick would be sweet as,' said Shortie. 'Somehow we've gotta find out who it is or we're all goin' to be in the shit.'

Tom knew he was right but that didn't make the job any easier.

'Set up a meeting Shortie—I wanna talk to the lads,' he said sitting forward in his seat. 'The grass has gotta be caught and we should be prepared to do anything to get him.'

* * *

The laundry department where Nick had been assigned was situated in a separate part of the prison well away from the induction wing, and to get there meant having to exit the main building and cross the exercise area. As Nick stepped out from his cell block, in the second group of prisoners being escorted to work that morning, the cold autumn air hit him full in the face. For a second he closed his eyes and savoured the feeling. He trailed behind the forty other prisoners, taking in as many deep breaths of the clean fresh air as he could, realising it was his fifth day in prison, but his first time out in the open.

The yard was deserted except for two prisoners sweeping up leaves and a few guards patrolling the perimeter fence. One of the prisoners put down his broom and wandered towards the laundry party, but he didn't get far before being called back by a guard holding onto a large Alsatian that was straining on his lead. It looked mean, hungry and ready for action.

Across the way, some fifty yards from the main gate Nick could see a white van being unloaded with its doors wide open. Two men were hauling off large packages and carrying them to the open doors at the back of a building. For a fleeting moment Nick toyed with the idea of making a run for it. He would hide in the back and wait for it to be driven away—just like in the movies. But he was only playing with the idea, he knew the dog would get to him before he could make it. He had once seen a police dog display at his old school where the dogs had been put into attack mode by a man acting as a burglar. The memory of the savage attack remained strong enough in Nick's mind to wipe out all thoughts of taking a chance. I wonder if anyone has escaped from here? he thought.

'Wood, keep up with the others,' shouted their escort. Nick quickened his step and latched himself firmly onto the back of the group.

As the group became closer to the laundry, Nick could see it out more clearly and it reminded him of one of the large warehouses on the industrial estate near his home, corrugated iron walls with flat top roofs, just a big metal box built on the cheap. Only problem with this metal box was that it was unbelievably hot and noisy inside.

As Nick stepped through the door the blast of hot air nearly took his breath away. No-one had warned him about the heat. He was hoping Jason could give him the rundown on what to expect at work but he'd done a disappearing act. When Nick had returned from the washroom that morning incredibly Jason was nowhere to be seen and the slop bucket had not been emptied. Nick had to do that... again.

He looked down at the overalls he was wearing on top of his prison shirt and sweater. Already he could feel himself starting to sweat but he didn't fancy stripping off outside the security of his cell and decided that he would put up with the discomfort.

Most of the inmates in Nick's group already had jobs in the laundry and went straight to their usual work places, but Nick was left standing with the three other prisoners that had been escorted with him to Blackthorpe. He'd not seen much of them since induction and only gave a cursory nod of greeting. The face of one of the inmates was badly bruised. It looked like Scarface had been in a fight.

A guard walked across to the small group. 'Any of you worked in a laundry before?' he asked. Nick looked at the other three but no-one spoke. He wondered if he should do the same but before he knew it he was following Jason's advice. 'I'm good at folding sheets, Guv.' Nick was thankful the guard didn't ask him exactly what experience he'd had. Instead, he ticked off a box on his clipboard. 'Okay Wood, report to the supervisor's office over there,' he said pointing to an area at the back of the laundry.

Nick looked across but couldn't see an office or a supervisor. All he could see was a mass of large machines. Perfect place for a mugger to hide, he thought. He looked back at the guard but he was already sorting out where Scarface should be allocated so he had no option but to make his way over.

Nick had never been in an industrial laundry before. He'd expected to see washing machines similar to those in a laundrette, but these were different. They were enormous, probably four times as big, and they had definitely seen better days. There must have been twenty of them, endlessly churning away. There were also about twenty hot air dryers stacked on top of each other which, by the sounds of it, had loose drums inside Clank—Clank—Clank. The noise was incredible and Nick could understand why some of the inmates working close to the biggest machines were wearing ear defenders. He put his hands over his ears to help drown out some of the volume but thought better of it when several inmates appeared and started to unload a machine that had finished it's cycle. It was probably best to suffer a perforated ear drum than be thought of as a wimp.

Nick gave the inmates a wide berth all the time, taking care to protect his back. Slowly he made his way along the avenue of machines to the far side of the room where he spotted a man wearing a white coat. 'Name and number?' yelled the supervisor when Nick was standing near enough to hear.

'Wood 582,' he shouted back. The supervisor made a note on his clipboard then turned away gesturing that Nick should follow. They walked behind another stack of machines to an open space where an inmate was slumped in a chair with his head resting on a table. The supervisor tapped the man on the shoulder. 'Your new helper,' he yelled pointing at Nick. 'Show him what to do'.

At first the man didn't look up. 'Hey, Smith, I'm talking to you!' persisted the supervisor. The man then turned his head round. Nick mouth dropped open in surprise—it was Jason. He hadn't recognised his friend because of the way he'd been slumped in the chair. When Jason wasn't asleep he was a lively person, full of 'get up and go'. He looked down at his cell mate in horror. Jason's face was white, his eyes were bloodshot and sweat poured from his brow. 'Hi,' said Nick forcing a smile. Jason gave him a blank look and turned away.

'Smith will show you what to do—won't you,' the supervisor said loudly.

Jason gave a barely perceptible nod. The man in the white coat shook his head. 'Liven up or I'll put you on report,' he said sternly. He looked back at Nick and shrugged. 'Just do as he says,' he shouted and with that, walked away.

When the supervisor was out of sight, Nick leaned on the table. 'Are you OK Jason?' he asked his friend. 'You look dreadful.'

'I'm 'cluckin',' he said. Nick looked at him blankly.

'Cluckin'—cold turkey,' he said impatiently. 'I need a fix bad.'

Nick now realised the stories he'd heard about people on heroin were true. The weekend bang up had given Nick a chance to work and get his picture finished, but there had been one or two moments when he'd wished he could have slept through the whole lot like Jason. But now seeing his friend in this state...

For a while Nick tried to make conversation but it was clear Jason wasn't interested. With his head resting on the table he told Nick what to do, then seemingly went to sleep. The task they were set wasn't complicated and Nick started to work on his own. A stack of unfolded sheets lay in a trolley to his left. He had to fold them up and then pile them onto a larger trolley which had to be wheeled to another department when it was full. With Jason incapable of doing anything, that wasn't likely for ages, but Nick worked hard to make sure the trolley was at least half stacked before the supervisor returned. It was boring work and Nick hated every minute. For two hours he grafted while Jason did as little as possible. At college he had often complained the work his tutors set was boring, but that morning he realised the true meaning of the word. It seemed an eternity had passed before a loud hooter announced it was time for a fifteen minute tea break.

Almost immediately the supervisor materialised, walked over to a nearby dry cleaning machine and turned it off. 'I'll be out to switch it on again in fifteen minutes. Don't touch it till I get back. Health and safety regulations,' he said wagging his finger.

He was just about to leave when Jason lifted his head. 'Guv I don't feel well. I think I've got flu,' he groaned.

'Flu,' said the supervisor with more than a hint of disgust in his voice. 'Is that what you call it?'

'Honest Guv, I think I'm going to be sick.'

The supervisor gave Jason a withering look. 'You want to go back to the wing do you?' he asked impatiently. Jason nodded without speaking. 'I'll have to go and see if there's an officer spare to take you back,' he said with undisguised irritation. 'You're no use to me as you are. You won't get paid if you miss work you know!'

Jason lay his head back on the table. 'I don't care—I just need to lie down,' he mumbled. The supervisor sighed, turned away and went in search of a guard.

'Why not just stay here,' said Nick, worried he was going to be left alone. 'I'll work quicker and you can sleep.'

'No,' said Jason. 'I've gotta get back to the wing.'

'Why?' asked Nick knowing that Jason needed all the pay he could get.

'Christ you're thick. Why do you think? I gotta get me a fix.'

'Where from?' asked Nick 'Everyone's at work.'

'Not the Dragon, it's Monday. The meat man delivered this morning. He'll 'ave been sorted by now. Amazing what comes with the pork pies.'

Nick heard footsteps approach and turned to see the supervisor and a guard. 'Right, Smith, off you go.' Jason levered himself up from the table and followed the guard with his feet dragging across the floor.

'You'll have to work on your own till lunch,' the supervisor said to Nick over his shoulder as he followed the guard to the entrance. Nick looked at the stack of sheets he had folded. You'll be lucky he thought to himself as sweat trickled down his back. I've done enough for today.

When the supervisor had disappeared Nick moved across to the table, sat down wearily on the chair and was just about to put his head down when he was grabbed by the back of his collar and hauled to his feet. Someone behind then shoved him forward, slamming him into a machine. A blinding pain exploded in his head as his chin hit the door. Instinctively he braced himself for the next onslaught. *Not again!* screamed a voice inside his head, but no blows reigned down. Slowly he turned to face his attacker and saw one of the Dragon's henchmen standing before him. Nick realised he was cowering like a frightened animal so trying to show some bravado he stood up to his full height. The man stepped forward. 'Got our money yet?' he said poking Nick hard in the chest.

'I don't need it till the end of the week,' said Nick at the same time as wondering if he had misunderstood when he had to pay.

'Just checking you haven't forgotten,' the man said. His hand then reached forward and steel-like fingers clamped onto Nick's chin. The pressure increased until Nick thought his teeth would break. 'Make sure you've got it Friday night. We don't want to 'ave to make an example of you.'

Then as instantly as the attack had started, the man smiled, his aggression evaporated and he wandered away whistling to himself. One minute the man was going to beat hell out of him, the next he looked like he was having a pleasant walk in the country. The guy's a fucking physco! thought Nick.

When the man was out of sight Nick collapsed in the chair. For several minutes he stayed locked in a trance while his imagination conjured up what would happen to him if he couldn't raise the money. It wasn't as though he had a chance of fighting back. He would get 'done' and 'done' bad. He would be made an example of for others to see. 'Look there goes Wood with those ugly scars. That's what happens if you can't pay the Dragon.'

Nick put his head in his hands. All this for selling a few fucking 'Es', he thought bitterly. Blackthorpe prison was his worst nightmare come to life. He sat deflated, wondering how he could possibly survive. He'd already been beaten up and he dreaded the thought of it happening again. He thought back to what Scarface had said about pouring boiling water over an inmate and wondered if it was only a grass that was punished in that way. Or would he simply be carved up with a knife. Perhaps they've got something really special waiting for me, he thought. He could only imagine the worst and the worst was as bad as it gets.

* * *

On the other side of the prison Tom Hawks sat at his table in the metal shop and took a sip of tea from his mug. The meeting had been arranged to take place during the tea break and he had now been joined by several other lifers. Some of them worked in other departments but they'd made their way across to join Tom for the fifteen-minute break.

'Enjoy the bang up?' asked one.

Tom looked across. There was no need to answer, there wasn't a lifer who wouldn't have suffered. Most of them had spent years keeping a clean sheet and they didn't appreciate having to pay for the mistakes of others. 'Something's gotta be done.' he said. 'We've gotta find this grass before the whole gaff erupts.'

'But how?' said another looking round at the same time as placing his drink on the table. As he withdrew his hand he accidently tipped over the mug, spilling tea everywhere. It was an everyday accident but the reaction was anything but.

One of the lifers leapt up—'Christ, watch what you're doin' you clumsy shit!' The inmate who had spilt the tea reacted instantly and crouched down ready to attack. As quick as a flash Shortie moved between the two men and broke off the confrontation—but the moment had left its mark on all present. There had been no trouble on the lifer's wing for months; no fights, no ill feeling. Tom couldn't remember the last time any of them had been caught for drugs or hooch, but cracks were starting to appear. Tom looked across at the two men who were now sitting down.

'We must stick together.' he said banging his fist on the table. 'We've all got contacts on the other wings—use them. Somewhere, someone is sending notes to the governor and we need to find out who,' said Tom. But deep down he knew that unless the grass made a stupid mistake, the chances of finding him were remote

Chapter 7

Nick didn't bother with lunch after his morning in the laundry, he was too nervous to eat. He'd told Amy Jones he would have a picture to show her on Monday and during lunchtime he got permission to visit the art department. The corridors were even more quiet than before and the art room was shut when he arrived. He waited impatiently outside but it wasn't long before Amy turned up. She nodded and smiled at Nick, unlocked the door and went in with him following behind. In the safety of the art room Nick took out his painting from underneath his shirt, where it had been stashed during the journey from his wing. Amy didn't smile at this elaborate precaution. She felt sad it was necessary but she knew that muggings were common place in the prison.

'Well done for finishing it so quickly,' she said hoping that Nick's work would not be too depressing and painted in the dark colours of despair. She held out her hand, took the painting from Nick and carefully unfurled it on the table in front of her. For a moment she said nothing as she tried to absorb the impact the painting had on her. It was brilliant and not just the stunning mix of bold, bright, colours that leapt off the paper, but it was beautifully painted with a high degree of skill. It was by far the best picture she had ever seen an inmate paint. Nick had hoped for a positive reaction and from the look of pleasure that spread across her face, he could tell she was impressed.

'This is very good Nick. You've got real talent,' she said at the same time as thinking, What a painful waste for it to be locked away in here.

Nick fidgeted impatiently as Amy looked more closely at his work. He wasn't interested in hearing compliments, all he wanted to know was would it help him earn some extra cash. 'Will it sell Miss?' he asked.

Amy hesitated. 'I can't guarantee it,' she said.

Worry clouded Nick's face as he pictured what would happen to him should he miss a payment. 'It's got to sell Miss, it's just got to,' he insisted.

Amy could see the worry etched on Nick's face, but there was little she could do to reassure him. 'It's not that simple,' she said. 'Visits are sometimes cancelled, sometimes there's hardly anybody there. Even though the picture's good, you've got to be lucky.'

Nick's look of worry turned to one of fear. 'If it doesn't sell Miss, I might as well kill myself.'

The tone of Nick's voice, the desperation carved in every syllable suddenly made Amy realise why he was panicking. Only physical danger made someone cringe in such a way. 'You need the money for protection don't you?' she said. Nick looked at the floor and nodded.

Amy sighed. There was nothing that upset her more than when young inmates were picked on by the bullies, but she knew it was no good trying to get Nick to tell her who was holding him to ransom. The fear of being labelled a grass kept mouths closed.

'I know someone who might frame it for you, make it look extra special,' she said trying to sound positive. Tom Hawks, one of her students from the lifer's wing had framed some of his own paintings in the past and she felt sure he would help out if she asked him to.

'That would be great Miss—anything to help it

sell. If it does, how do I get the money?' I've got to have it by Friday night.'

'It's transferred straight into your account. Normally I'd be able to tell you straight away but I'm away this week. You'll have to wait till you collect your pay at canteen.' Amy felt compelled to offer her opinion even though she knew the probable reaction. 'Can't you tell an officer about this?' she asked.

Nick stood looking at her wondering if she could possibly understand the trouble he was in. He faced a stark choice; boiling water over the nuts from Scarface for grassing, or being scarred for life by the Dragon.

'No miss,' he said opting to suffer a slashed face instead of boiled bollocks. The dark side of his sense of humour suddenly made him burst out with laughter. He wondered how the people who thought that prison is a holiday camp would advertise the option in their brochure. A spa treatment or a facial.

'What's the matter?' asked Amy.

'I don't think you'd get it Miss,' replied Nick.

Minutes later, back in the world of the living nightmare, he walked to his cell with more paper carefully rolled under his shirt. If he did make it through Friday he would need to finish another painting for the following week.

* * *

On his way back to the wing, Nick passed the canteen where the inmates were finishing off lunch. He peered through the window in the hope that food was still being served but he saw that everything had been cleared away and the servers had disappeared. The canteen itself however, was busier than normal with all the tables full, and Nick guessed that the meal had been a good one for a change. Just my luck, he thought.

For once, not having to worry about muggers on

the way, he walked the last few yards to the staircase looking at the notices hanging on the walls. Most of them were illegible and covered with thrown food, the ones he did bother to read were a joke: No music to be played after lights out. Yeah right.

But his spirits lifted when he saw the normally packed phone booths standing empty. All of a sudden he got the crazy idea of phoning Jessica. Why not? he thought. I've got nothing to lose. A surge of adrenaline shot through his body as he pictured Jessica at home. Without thinking twice, he raced up the stairs to his cell, retrieved his phone card and before he knew it was back downstairs where furtively he slipped into a booth. He had not been allowed to speak to her since the accident and she'd made no attempts to get in touch with him, but right now, none of that mattered.

The phones were almost identical to the public phones in the outside world and without wasting time Nick slipped his card into the slot and from memory tapped out Jessica's X directory number. It only rang a few times before someone answered. 'Hello.' Nick recognised the voice of their housekeeper.

'Hi, can I speak to Jessica please?' There was a moment's pause.

'Who is speaking?'

'Just a friend. It's really important,' he said.

This time the reply sounded rehearsed. 'I'm afraid the family have gone away for a month. They won't be back until...' but Nick had heard enough. Jessica's father had made it clear to him he was not to contact his daughter again and he'd obviously left instructions with the maid. He couldn't even try Jessica's mobile phone, that was the first thing her father had destroyed.

He hung up the receiver feeling frustrated and crushingly alone, when he heard a voice calling him.

'Hey, Wood! I want to talk to you.' He knew it

wasn't a guard—the office had been closed. He risked a glance round and saw it was Scarface. Shit! He pretended he hadn't seen or heard him, just moved off casually and when out of sight, bolted up the stairs taking two at a time. He ignored Scarface when he called out again. 'Wood! I need a phone card.'

Jason's words came into his mind. 'Never borrow, never lend.' Nick knew that if Scarface caught up with him, he would submit and give up his one card. He knew he had to hide quickly. He turned right onto the second landing and went through the entrance door. He hesitated for a second before moving forward as the passage ahead was dark.

'Wood! I know you're there. Wait for me.'

No way, thought Nick. He could hear Scarface's footsteps hurrying up the stairs and without having time to let his eyes adjust to the gloom, he quickly made his way down the corridor past rows of locked cells. Then, at the end of the corridor, he was confronted by a heavy metal door. Don't panic, he told himself, just think. He guessed the door would lead onto another wing. There was bound to be more than one way out. Just then Scarface's gravely voice called out again.

'Wood, you're pissing me off.'

Nick pushed hard against the door and it swung open. He slipped through, risking a quick glance behind him and then pushed the door closed hoping Scarface might not have seen. With his back to the door he turned round to see where he was and stared into a long dark corridor that looked like hell itself.

Someone had painted the strip lighting dark red. It's dim glow made it impossible to see clearly and there were no windows giving light from the outside. A putrid smell was coming from two bins just to his right which were full to over flowing with rotting food, and dirty plates and cups lay scattered on the floor. Three corridors faced him, one to the right, one to the left and one straight ahead. Trying to ignore the stench Nick made his way forward. He heard someone to his right hawk up and gob out the phlegm. As his eyes became used to the gloom, he could see a man slouched against the wall to his left where the washroom would be. He was huge and his head was turned in Nick's direction. Nick tried to calm himself, thinking just keep going and don't look round.

He looked towards the end of the corridor that faced him and he could now see a door. He hurried towards it hoping that safety lay beyond. All the time his ears strained to hear the sound of Scarface. As he reached the next door his imagination went into overdrive. Where the fuck am I heading now? he thought. Hoping he wasn't about to swap this landing for something worse, he stretched out his hand to grab the handle when his luck ran out. A hand shot out from a cell on the right and grabbed him by the arm. Nick crumbled to his knees.

'Get in 'ere quick,' came a voice. Nick's heart was thumping so hard at first he didn't recognise the voice. Then he looked more closely at the silhouetted body. 'Jason is that you?' he said in a loud whisper. 'Scarface is after me.'

'Yeah. I know,' he said dragging Nick into the cell.

Once inside Jason took hold of the table and pushed it against the door, 'If he comes in smash him over the head with this,' he said giving Nick a solid looking piece of wood.

'I can't,' said Nick in a complete state of panic. 'I've never hit anyone.'

'It's easy,' said Jason. 'Do it or we're dead men.' The boys put their ears close to the door to listen. They could hear footsteps coming fast towards them— and then they knew Scarface was outside.

'Wood, where the fuck are yer?' he shouted.

'Where the fuck 'av you gone?'

For a moment they thought the door would come flying open but after what seemed an eternity they heard the door at the end of the corridor open. For moments they stood straining to hear any noise but finally Jason whispered, 'I think he's gone. We're in the clear.'

Nick dropped the piece of wood to the ground and sank onto a nearby chair. He looked across at his friend, 'I owe you,' he said.

'Too fuckin' right you do,' said Jason breaking into a grin.

Nick shook his head in disbelief, staggered his friend could smile. 'What the hell is this place?' he asked. 'It's like zombie land.'

'It's the smack 'ead's landing, the screws hardly ever come 'ere. Not much point. No-one's gonna do what they say. This is a mate's cell.'

Concerned Scarface might come back Nick stood up and went over to the door. It was still quiet outside and with no sound of the frustrated lunatic, he turned round feeling a little more relaxed.

'Scarface wanted my phone card,' he said explaining the chase. But then his mind switched to the problem of where they were. 'How do people survive here?' he asked in amazement.

'It's ok once you know the ropes. Anyway, it's easy to get hold of the gear up 'ere,' said Jason emptying out his pockets. He then turned to his friend. 'Nick mate, I need your help. Time to repay me for saving your life.'

Warning bells started ringing in Nick's ears. 'What do you want me to do?' he asked watching Jason fumbling with some toilet roll. 'I'm not doing anything dodgy, Jason. I'm sorry but...'

'I need you to help me take a fix,' interrupted his friend.

'No way!' gasped Nick. But Jason didn't seem to hear or chose not to, and continued rolling the tissue into a tight roll about three feet long.

'We can't get hold of needles in here so we 'chase the dragon'.'

Nick shook his head. He'd only heard the expression once before and that was on a television programme about desperate drug addicts. 'Jason,' he pleaded. 'I don't need this kind of trouble.'

'It's not trouble Nick, you're just doing a favour for a friend.'

Jason then stuffed one end of the rolled up paper into Nick's hand and before he could argue he turned back to the cupboard and took down a carefully prepared piece of foil.

'You've gotta hold the light under the foil understand?' he said as he flicked on his lighter and set fire to one end of the roll of tissue paper Nick was holding. It became like a giant match. Jason then put something onto the foil, moved it over the flame and with his other hand picked up the empty tube of a biro.

Within a few moments the small brown piece of heroin was spitting and bubbling across the surface. Jason looked Nick in the eye. 'Get it?' he said. 'Chasing the dragon.'

He then turned his attention to the job in hand, put the biro tube to his lips and let the other end follow the heroin as it skitted across the foil. Time after time he inhaled deeply. The taper was so tightly rolled it burned slowly and it seemed to take forever before the heroin had been boiled away. After he had sucked up the Dragon's last breath Jason stood swaying on his feet. The biro tube fell from his hand. He tried to speak but Nick couldn't understand a word and his eyes had glazed over. Jason tried to put his hand on Nick's shoulder but missed, and the momentum of his swinging arm made him overbalance and he fell onto the bed.

Nick bent down to see if he was all right but Jason's hand reached up and grabbed his arm.

'Tha. . Than… Thanks,' he said.

Nick's mind sped back over the months to the nightmare evening when Jessica had collapsed in front of him. He looked down at his friend wondering what to do. He felt numb. He took hold of Jason's shirt in his hands.

'Are you ok? Are you OK?' he shouted shaking his friend with frustration. Jason's glazed eyes looked back at him and there was a slight smile on his lips. Nick felt tears filling his eyes. He knew that he had to do something. He couldn't leave Jason there on his own, not with Scarface charging about. And he knew Jason would be in real trouble if the screws found him in such a drugged up state. He would have to get him back to his cell and make it look as if Jason was ill.

He pulled the table away from the door and took a peep outside to see if the coast was clear. Scarface was nowhere to be seen and the corridor seemed empty.

'Jason, pull yourself together. We've got to get out of here.' Jason started murmuring and attempted to get to his feet but fell back onto the bed. Nick grabbed his arm and levered him upright.

'Come on, wake up or I'm leaving you here,' he said threateningly, at the same time as knowing he wasn't going to leave his friend anywhere.

'Okay, okay,' slurred Jason.

Nick managed to get him to his feet. 'Come on for Christ's sake,' he said. But he realised his friend was incapable of walking. Nick pulled Jason's arm round his neck and hauled him roughly towards the door. Once more he checked outside. 'Hang on to me and keep quiet,' he said.

Outside in the corridor Nick retraced his steps, dragging Jason with him all the way back to their wing, where he managed to haul Jason up the flight of stairs to their landing. He hesitated at the top when he saw two inmates in conversation halfway between them and the cell but quickly realised he had no choice but to carry on past. He struggled to keep Jason on his feet but neither of the men seemed to notice Nick's predicament—or more likely chose not to.

'Come on, Jason, keep going. We're nearly there,' Nick whispered—but as soon as the words were out of his mouth, he heard a guard coming up the stairs behind them. Nick realised there wasn't enough time to reach their cell so he bundled Jason into the nearby washroom.

'Fuck's sake shut up and stand still,' he said to Jason roughly. For what seemed an age he propped Jason up against a sink while he strained his ears to hear any footsteps outside. When all seemed quiet he opened the door, took a quick look down the landing and deciding to trust his luck, he dragged Jason out of the washroom and along the corridor to their cell.

Inside, Nick kicked the pulled the door closed behind him and dropped Jason onto the bottom bunk. It had taken all his strength to get him back and sweat was dripping from his brow. He knew it must be almost time to return to work, but before he disappeared he wanted to make sure Jason was all right. He bent over and listened to his friend breathing, but as he bent down something stuck into his ribs. He reached inside his shirt and took out the paper Amy had given him. It was creased and without careful attention not much use. He tossed it at the table in disgust. So this is what friends are for, he thought.

Suddenly he heard footsteps outside. Louder and louder they became until they stopped right outside the cell. Nick froze. At first he thought it might be Scarface and he braced himself for an attack, but the man who entered was wearing a uniform.

'I've come to see the inmate that reported in sick,' said the officer. 'This him then?' he said pointing at Jason.

'I think he's got flu, Guv,' said Nick trying to calm his heavy breathing.

The officer walked across to the bottom bunk. 'Got the flu have you?' he asked.

Jason was silent. In the safety of his own cell he had simply crashed out.

The officer looked at Jason's eyes and then, bending over the body, smelt his breath. He glanced round at Nick. 'I've been in the service long enough to know the difference between a bad cold and a 'tripper' he said. 'This man's been taking heroin. You been helping him have you? You'd better turn out your pockets, Wood,' he said giving Nick a cold stare.

There was no point in protesting and Nick emptied his pockets onto the table. The officer rummaged through the bits of paper but there was nothing there to implicate him.

'Looks like you're lucky this time Wood, but I'll be watching you from now on. I can't stand smack 'eads and this lad's been on the gear.'

Nick thought the officer had finished with him and he turned to go but he was called back. 'Aren't you in for dealing drugs?' the officer asked with a look of disgust on his face.

Nick's face turned bright red, 'It was only the once... and I don't do drugs.'

The officer gave him a scornful look. 'If I had my way I'd lock the like's of you up and throw away the key,' he said.

With his head hung low and his self esteem in tatters Nick drifted back to work, not even caring if he bumped into Scarface on the way.

* * *

Tom Hawks was getting ready to return to work when a phone call came through to the guard's office on the lifer's wing. Amy Jones wanted to see him and he was not to go to work until she arrived. Tom was quite happy about that as lunch, for once, had been pretty good and he'd eaten as much as he could. For a few minutes he sat and waited in the lifer's canteen. He'd known Amy for over a year now. At first he couldn't believe it when she gave a special art class to the lifers. Most of the education staff were a bit apprehensive of doing that, but Amy had turned out to be a real gem.' Tom had attended the first class and had become hooked.

He looked up as he heard someone enter the deserted canteen. Amy breezed in holding something in her hands. Tom got up as she approached but she waved him back down, walked up to the table and unfurled Nick's painting.

'What do you think?' she asked.

Tom stared down at the picture. He'd grown a thick skin in prison. He rarely thought about the outside world, to be honest he couldn't really remember it all that well. The gray drab surrounds of the prison walls were now his home. But looking down at the painting in front of him brought memories flooding back that had been buried for years. It was the nearest he'd come to tasting freedom since he'd been banged up and it took him several seconds before he managed to regain the control of his thoughts.

'Who the hell did this?' he asked.

'One of the new inmates who arrived last week—young man—boy really, called Nick Wood.'

Tom thought back to when he had seen the last batch of inmates arrive. 'Small, thin kid with blond hair?' he asked. Amy nodded.

'Well, I'll be,' he said. 'He certainly works fast.'

At first Amy had been apprehensive about giving separate art classes to the lifers but it wasn't long after meeting Tom, Shortie and the others that she realised the myth surrounding them was just a myth. They'd worked hard, listened to her advice and were always polite. She felt the ones she had met could be trusted and now she needed Tom's help.

'He needs money Tom, he's under pressure to pay off someone for protection. He wants to see if he can sell his pictures in the visits hall and I wondered if you could frame this one for me? Give it a better chance.'

Tom studied the picture again. He would have given anything to have been able to paint a picture as good as this one. He looked at the brilliant colours and wondered at the talent needed to produce something so powerful from behind the prison walls. 'It'll need better wood than I've got to do it justice,' he said.

Amy smiled. "I'll get you anything you want Tom,' she said knowing there was no better man in the prison to do the job. 'I've got to go now,' she said getting up. 'Any chance of having it finished by Thusday? It's the first time we could get it on show?'

Back in his cell Tom rested the picture on his bed and stood back to study it again. He rubbed his chin and nodded his approval. For minutes he gazed at the picture oblivious to anything else, even the footsteps that approached from outside. It was Officer Les Wright that poked his head round the door. 'Ready to go to work now?' he asked.

Tom nodded but then pointed at the picture. 'What do you think of this?' he asked.

Les looked towards the painting. He didn't know much about art but he liked what he saw. 'That's really good,' he said moving nearer to take a closer look. 'You're improving,' he said.

'Wish I were,' said Tom. 'But it's not mine. A

new kid called Wood did it. The kid I asked you about'

Les thought for a minute. 'The one who came in with Scarface?'

Tom nodded. 'Talented little bugger ain't he. Amy said he needs some dosh and wants to try and sell this in the visits hall. She's asked me to frame it.'

'It might go,' said Les. 'Better than most I've seen.'

'It'll definitely go,' said Tom standing back to admire the picture one last time before picking up his coat. 'Keep an eye on him for me will you?' he asked Les. 'A kid that can paint like this has got to have some good in him. Worth looking after don't you think?' For the first time in days Tom walked to work thinking about something other than catching the grass.

Chapter 8

On Tuesday morning Nick woke up in the top bunk. The night before he'd tried to move his friend but it had proved impossible and Nick had climbed up to spend a restless night on a mattress that was harder and more lumpy than his own. He tried stretching out his back, sore from hauling Jason all over the prison and then lay back to doze.

So much had happened so quickly, he hadn't had much time to miss home or his freedom, but as he lay in bed that morning he realised how much he was missing both. It staggered him how quickly his life had fallen apart; from a bright future as an artist to the hell in Blackthorpe. He mentally kicked himself for bothering to call Jessica. He wouldn't be doing that again. It was beginning to dawn on him what a fool he'd been. His life had now changed forever.

There was no way he could go back to anything he had known before, not after all this. The only thing he hoped he could rely on was his mum and sister.

He wondered about his mum and hoped his sister was giving her the support she probably needed. He also hoped that soon they might visit. He still hadn't received a reply to his letter, but apparently that didn't mean much. Everything had to be inspected before being handed to the prisoners and sometimes it took days before the mail came through.

From the bottom bunk Nick heard Jason cough. Finally he had woken up. 'I feel the pits,' he said slowly coming round. 'Where am I?'

'In my bloody bunk.'

Nick wasn't sure how much his cell mate remembered so he gave him a brief account of the previous day's exploits. When he'd finished, Jason stuck out his head. 'Thanks, I owe you,' he said coughing up a large piece of phlegm and gobbing it into the slop bucket. 'But don't worry about Scarface, he'd have found himself a fix somehow. He'll feel as bad as me and won't remember a thing. Now leave me alone. I feel like shit.'

Serve you right, thought Nick, who was still smarting at Jason. 'Don't ask me again Jason,' he said firmly. 'I won't do it.'

There was an embarrassed silence. Nick swung his legs out of bed, clambered down to the floor and headed out to the washroom.

* * *

Deep inside the prison an inmate was waiting for his cell mate to go down for breakfast. When he was finally alone, he blocked the door with the table making sure no one could disturb him. The night before, he had overheard a conversation and learned some information he had to pass on to the governor. One of the lifers wanted to buy some hooch for the weekend. It was being smuggled to him at work on Friday morning. He thought back to the time when he had been caught stealing from another man's cell and had taken a severe beating from the lifers. His jaw tensed as he re-lived the pounding blows. His attackers had thought it was a sufficient lesson and had kept quiet about the incident. Weak bastards thought the man, grinding his fist into his hand. There was a flicker of amusement in his eyes as he wrote out the note. For once he wasn't concerned about the favours he might get. Revenge came in its sweetest form whenever he could grass up a lifer.

Suddenly there was a knock on the door. The man quickly folded the note and stuffed it in his pocket. It would be curtains for him if anyone ever found him out. He pulled the table away from the door just as a guard from downstairs poked his head round. 'Governor wants to see you,' he said.

'What about?' asked the man.

'Investigation into how that inmate got beaten up the other week.' he said.

The man smiled; for once it had nothing to do with him. 'The governor's in a right mood. You'd better look smart,' said the guard.

'Give me a second then.' The man got up and from his cupboard took out a clean pair of jeans he had just got back from the laundry. Won't even have to bother with the note now, he thought, I can tell the Governor myself. He quickly took off the dirty pair of jeans, slung them in his wash bag and slipped on the clean pair. Looking good enough for a day in church, he thought to himself as he walked out.

* * *

On his way back from having breakfast, Nick stopped off at the guard's office in the wild hope that there might be a letter for him. He looked down the list scribbled on the board outside the office. At first he couldn't believe it when he saw his name and thought there was probably another inmate called Wood, but after checking the number scrawled by the side he realised someone had written to him. 'There's a letter for me Guv, Wood 582.'

The officer who was handing out the mail looked through the pile, drew one out and without speaking, handed it over. Nick took the letter and slipped it straight into his pocket. He was learning fast and was already becoming accustomed to hiding everything from prying eyes

When he got back to the cell he found Jason had disappeared, and alone with the door pulled shut, he took out his letter. He stared at his sister's large confident handwriting and wondered why it was Lisa and not his mum who had written first. Maybe there was a problem at home. Maybe his mum had been taken ill after all the stress he'd put her through. There was only one way to find out. He tore open the envelope and with a sick feeling in his stomach, he read the first page.

Dear Brother, (huh bet you never thought you'd hear me call you dear!)....

Nick smiled. His sister was two years younger than himself but always talked and acted as if she was ten years older. There had been times when he could have strangled her with his bare hands, but not anymore. Amazingly, since he'd been in trouble she'd been a star.

His eyes quickly scanned the first lines.

... everything at home is fine, mum says to tell you she'll write tomorrow. Well, how are you feeling I hope that you have got a nice room and are on your own—I'd hate to have to share but perhaps it isn't too bad if your room mate is OK...

It was obvious that Lisa had no idea of the state of Her Majesty's prisons but who could blame her; he probably would have written something similar to one of his friends.

The letter wasn't newsy, and it wasn't long, but it asked how he was and showed genuine concern. More importantly it told Nick that Lisa and his mother would be visiting him on Thursday. Nick punched the air with delight. Only two days to go until he saw them again. And hopefully they'll see my picture on display, he thought. Maybe they could even buy it. For the first time since arriving in prison Nick's face split into a wide grin.

* * *

Only two hours of the morning shift had passed at work but Nick felt he had been folding sheets for an eternity. At least he'd had someone to talk to. Jason wasn't nearly as bad as he had been after the weekend bang up when all he could do was sleep, and being able to chat had helped pass the time. But it was a job Nick had now crossed off his 'to do' list. When the tea break hooter sounded he slumped down on one of the chairs and expected Jason to do likewise, but instead his cellmate picked up a bag off the floor and pulled out some clothes.

'They yours?' asked Nick.

Jason shook his head. 'The Dragon's. I collected them this morning. It'll help pay off the cash I owe 'im.'

Nick watched as Jason put his hands into the pockets of the jeans and dug out some mangy looking tissues and a piece of folded paper. He threw the tissues into the waste bin nearby, but he unfolded the piece of paper.

'Anything interesting?' asked Nick.

Jason hesitated while he stared at the paper. 'Nothing,' he said eventually, tossing it into the bin with the tissues. Jason then stuffed the clothes back in the bag. 'Be back in a minute, just gotta deal with this lot,' he said nodding at the bag of clothes.

Even though he was becoming used to the ever-present danger, Nick felt ill at ease while his friend was gone. All the time he nervously looked round in case the nutter who had attacked him the day before, came back to dish out another warning and he was relieved when Jason returned.

'Just had to take them over to a mate who bungs them in a washer for me,' he said sitting down. He got out his tobacco and rolled himself a cigarette. 'So how's the painting going?'

'The one I finished goes on show for Thursday visits. Amy Jones, the art teacher, says it's got a chance of selling.'

Jason hadn't seen the finished picture and had no idea if Nick was exaggerating his talent, the way most cons did and decided to put him to the test. 'How about drawing me then?' he said throwing down the gauntlet.

Nick shrugged. He enjoyed sketching faces and Jason would be a good subject. 'Okay but you've got to get me some paper and something to draw with,' he said.

Jason thought for a second then went over to the bin and dug out the folder piece of paper he'd found in the Dragon's pocket. He straightened it out and placed it clean side up on the table. Then he went over to the supervisor's office and grabbed a biro from the window ledge.

Nick pulled his chair across to the table, sat down and studied his subject. Jason looked good considering the state he was in the night before. He hadn't thought his cellmate would be capable of making it into work, but it seemed he'd made a miraculous recovery. 'How do you do it?' he asked shaking his head.

'Do what?'

'Recover from the state you were in yesterday?'

Jason shrugged. 'That was nothing, not compared to last weekend. Anyway, I managed to see my friend the doc this morning, he sorted me out with a couple of uppers.'

Nick stared at him. 'You mean the doctor knows about your habit and helps you out?'

'Don't be stupid! I'm suffering from depression aren't I?'

Jason feigned a forlorn expression and looked as though he was just about to burst into tears. 'He thinks I need anti-depressants to keep me from committing suicide. It happens a lot in prison, suicide.'

Jason noticed Nick's expression. 'Cheer up Nick. Don't you go getting depressed. Don't want them wasting their pills on the likes of you,' he said, lifting up his chin. 'Let's not waste time. Which do you think is my best side?'

Five minutes later Nick put down the pen. 'Right that's it. Best I can do in the time. I've got to go to the loo,' he said getting up from the table and walking off in the direction of the washroom.

Jason got up, picked up the drawing, and after a few seconds grinned. The cheeky bastard, he's takin' the piss! Nick had given him extra large ears and eyes like a Chinaman—just as good as the ones they do in the West End, he thought looking at the caricature. There weren't too many things in prison that made Jason smile so he decided to keep the drawing, folded it up and slipped it his pocket. At the same time a sixth sense made him wheel round but for once, even for Jason, there was no time for escape.

'Where is it, Smith?' the Dragon said menacingly.

Jason backed away. 'Where's what?' he said, desperately trying to think what the Dragon could be talking about.

'Don't play the innocent with me. Now hand it over.'

Jason stood in stunned silence. He had no idea what the Dragon could want.

'Right said the Dragon. 'I'll have to get it myself then.'

Jason didn't have time to avoid the first punch. The brass knuckle duster flashed out and thundered into his face just below his nose. A fountain of blood erupted from his mouth. His legs crumpled and he went tumbling to the ground. Instinctively he curled himself up into a ball as the Dragon's boot pounded into his side. Then one hard blow caught him on the side of the head and he passed out.

Nick fastened up his overalls as he walked out of the loo. He knew the tea break was almost over and he didn't want to be late back. He made his way through the maze of machines, along to his own section and was just about to enter the clearing when he spotted the Dragon bent over his friend. He appeared to be searching Jason's pockets. Nick had no idea what had happened but Jason appeared to be unconscious and a whole spectrum of thoughts bombarded him at the same time. He couldn't go in and stop the Dragon himself, he'd get beaten to pulp, but he had to do something. He looked round and spotted the 'start up' button on the machine to his right. Without thinking, his finger flashed out and hit it. Immediately the machine came to life and the relative quiet was shattered.

Hidden from view Nick watched the Dragon. Startled by the sudden noise, he'd leapt to his feet and without looking round, had made his escape between the stack of machines. When he was out of sight, Nick rushed over to where his friend lay motionless.

'Who switched that bloody machine on?' came an angry voice from over his shoulder. Nick heard heavy footsteps come up behind him and then suddenly the supervisor saw the body on the floor. Blood was flowing freely from Jason's smashed mouth. 'Did you do this?' he demanded.

'No, Guv,' said Nick.

'Well, who the hell did then?'

Nick realised he couldn't tell the truth and get himself into more trouble with the Dragon. 'Don't know, Guv,' he said. 'I was coming back from the toilet when I heard the machine start up and I found Smith lying here.'

The supervisor looked closely at Jason who was still not moving. 'Go and fetch a guard. Tell him we need a doctor—quick,' he ordered.

Nick ran off to the main entrance where the guards were stationed. Moments later he returned with a guard following on his heels. 'I phoned the medic. He'll be here soon,' said the officer, crouching down to inspect the injured man. Jason was now moving but coughing up blood.

'Lie still sonny,' said the supervisor with obvious concern. By the time the medic arrived there was a large pool of blood around Jason's head.

Once the medic had started to attend to Jason, the officer turned to the inmates who had gathered round the scene. 'Right you lot,' he roared just as a klaxon announced an early end to the morning's shift. 'I want you all back on your wings.'

Nick turned away with the others, but was called back by the guard. 'The governor will want to speak to you later, Wood,' he said. 'You'd better stay in your cell until we get you. And I should consider telling the truth about all this if I were you. If you saw who did this you'd better say. The Governor won't take lightly to you sticking to that bullshit story of yours.'

As he wandered back to the wing with the other prisoners escorted by four guards Nick realised he was in big trouble. He knew he should tell the truth and grass up the Dragon, but he knew his life wouldn't be worth living if he did. Nick wasn't a religious person but if he was, he would have said a prayer.

* * *

Officer Les Wright knocked on Tom's door during the lunch break and entered the cell. He found Tom sizing up several pieces of wood that had been dropped off at the lifer's wing by Amy. 'Don't know if you'll be needing that frame,' he said. 'Nick Wood's in a bit of trouble—shouldn't be surprised if he's gone by the morning.'

'What's happened?' asked Tom looking up.

'Someone got beaten up bad in the laundry this morning. They reckon Wood saw who did it.'

'Hope the kid's got enough sense to keep his mouth shut.'

Les shook his head, 'You know what the governor's like, he's bound to get the information out of him sooner or later. Once he does the kid will have to go.'

Tom knew Les was right. He'd be labelled a grass and Nick would be moved for his own safety. 'Good riddance if you ask me though,' said Les. 'The duty guard says he was helping his cellmate 'fix' yesterday.'

Tom looked surprised. 'You sure?' he said to Les. 'That doesn't sound like the young man Amy describes.' Tom was pretty sure that if Nick was a 'smack ead' Amy would have spotted it. There's a haunted look in the eyes of men on the gear but even so he decided to keep his options open and was prepared to listen to what Les had to say. 'You'd better tell me what happened,' he said.

Les pulled up a chair, took out his cigarettes and offered one to Tom. For the next few minutes he described the events of the morning. 'He's up before the governor sometime this afternoon,' he said finishing off the account. Tom didn't answer. The governor was like a barrister and could extract facts you didn't know existed. That would be the end of young Wood, and the last painting Tom would see.

For twenty years Tom had survived without ever asking an officer for a favour but at long last he decided to take a risk. He stubbed out his cigarette and lent forward in his chair. 'Les, I want you to do something for me,' he said hoping that it was a decision he wouldn't regret.

* * *

Two hours after lunch Nick was collected from his cell and escorted to the far side of the prison. He waited with the guard outside the Governor's office and at precisely two o'clock the officer knocked on the door. They waited until they heard a stern voice tell them to enter.

'Wood 582, sir,' announced the guard as he escorted Nick inside the room. Nick looked at the governor sitting behind his desk. He was smaller than Nick had imagined. He had a thin, gaunt face with hollow cheeks, a nose that was too long and pencil-thin lips. It looked to Nick as if he'd been chiselled out of ice. Covering his rather emaciated body was a navy blue suit that showed up the dandruff on the collar. He tried telling himself to keep calm but standing in the governor's office he went from worrying about Jason, to wishing he was the one in hospital, unconscious and out of it.

The governor looked up. 'For a new boy you've got yourself in trouble pretty quickly 582,' he said.

'I haven't done anything wrong, Guv,' he answered.

'You call the governor, Sir,' snapped the officer standing at his side.

The governor looked down at a sheet of paper on his desk and signed it. 'On the contrary, 582, you've done everything wrong. You have committed a crime for which you are being punished in prison, and now you are suspected of aiding an assault on a fellow prisoner.'

Nick was momentarily stunned. He thought he had been called as a witness, not as a suspect. 'Do you know what extra time you serve if found guilty of aiding an assault?'

Nick didn't answer.

'Up to two years... Think about that 582... Two more years in prison.'

The governor's cold eyes bored into the back of Nick's head. It felt as though his mind was being read. 'I went to the toilet, sir,' he explained in a rather unconvincing voice. 'When I got back the machine was on and I saw Smith lying on the floor.'

'So you never touched the machine then?'

'No Sir,' replied Nick.

'You're lying,' snapped the governor. 'Lie to me again and I'll dock your wages for the next month.'

'But you can't do that sir—I need the money.'

'Why, do you take drugs, 582?' asked the governor as quick as a flash. 'Or is it for something else?'

Nick had to think fast. He couldn't tell the governor it was to pay off the Dragon. 'I need money for my mother's birthday, Sir. I want to buy her a jewellery box from the woodwork department,' he said. Nick had thought that sticking to his story would be simple but now he felt he was digging himself into a hole. The governor grunted however and seemed to have accepted the story. Nick relaxed a little.

'Do you know what we did at lunch time, 582?' Nick shook his head, not sure if he was meant to answer. 'We had the machine in the laundry dusted for fingerprints—and guess who's were on it?' the governor said.

Nick was dumbstruck. He had no idea they

would, or in fact could, go to such lengths, but now they had him over a barrel. Now he'd got to tell the truth. If he didn't name the attacker he would be labelled as an accessory and end up doing more time. He opened his mouth to speak but suddenly there was a knock on the door.

'Who's that?' snapped the Governor. The door opened and officer Les Wright entered the room. Behind him was an inmate, tall, thick set, very pale skin. 'Sorry to trouble you, Sir,' said Les. 'You said that if we heard anything about the assault we should report it to you.'

The governor looked impatiently at the officer, but he had sent out a memo saying as much. 'Very well?' he asked. 'What is it?'

'Prisoner 212, says he's got vital information, Sir.'

The governor sighed. 'Come on in then,' he said looking at Pete Vacanni. 'Whatever it is, it had better be good.'

'It's about the assault Sir. I'm a witness as well you see, Sir. I was in the toilet along with Wood. I saw everything he saw so I thought you'd like to see me as well.'

Nick was stunned, as he'd never seen the man before. He certainly hadn't been in the washroom with him. He wasn't sure what was happening but it didn't matter anyway. They still had his fingerprints and could prove that Nick was somehow involved.

'So you're a witness as well are you?' said the governor with a sneer.

'Yes Sir. We were both having a slash when the machine started up. Nearly wet me boots thinking it was that time already. I said so sir,' continued the inmate. 'I said I didn't think it was time for the machine to start up. I hurried out of the bog, just in time to see the back of a bloke running off—dark hair and a limp he had. I guess he was the one who started the machine.' Then the inmate raised his voice. 'Pity they wiped the button clean before lunch or they could've got fingerprints.'

It was not a subtle message and Nick understood straight away. He had no idea why the man should be helping him out, but help him out he had. The governor had been bluffing. There were no fingerprints. Another minute and Nick would have blurted out the truth and been in real trouble.

He looked at the governor to see his reaction. He sat stone faced except for a nerve that twitched on the side of his left cheek 'Most enlightening, 212,' he said, clearly not amused. He turned to the officer. 'Take him outside and wait.'

When the door closed behind them the governor rose to his feet and stroked his chin. 'How come you never mentioned there was someone else in the lavatory? Surely it would have been in your interest to have said someone was with you when the machine was switched on?'

Nick decided that silence was his best defence and kept his eyes firmly fixed on the picture on the opposite wall, and observed that the Queen had aged considerably since the photo had been taken. The governor walked around him the way a shark circles his prey. 'Someone's come to your aid 582, but let me tell you, if someone's willing to stick their neck out for you that far, believe me, you'll be paying back big time.'

He looked at the officer and nodded his head. 'You can go now, Wood. You've had your chance to come clean and you've blown it. From now on don't come crying to me when you're in real trouble.'

Nick walked out of the office and thanked his lucky stars that he'd kept his mouth shut. He'd been so close to breaking. Why should anyone want to help me? he asked himself. He also wondered if the governor was right and there would be a price to pay.

* * *

Tom Hawks was reading at his table on the lifer's wing when the door opened. He raised his eyes and then put down his book. Les hovered by the door. 'Just popped up to tell you things seemed to have worked out. Governor wasn't too pleased when his plan was scuppered, but no real trouble. Looks like the kid's in the clear.'

Tom nodded his satisfaction. 'Thanks Les, I owe you.'

Les shook his head. 'No you don't, Tom. This one's on me,' he said, grinning as he closed the door behind him.

Tom could see that Les was tickled pink to get one over on the governor. The Grim Reaper would be disappointed not to get another conviction and worse still, another unsolved assault would blight his prison record. But a young man might have been saved from real problems and Les had helped.

Tom had suggested Les use Pete Vacanni to help rescue Nick Wood. He was an old campaigner when it came to dealing with prison governors and the plan had worked. Tom imagined the look on the governor's face when Vacanni gave his speil. In the short term they had saved the boy, but to help keep him safe, Tom had asked Les to help sort out one or two other things. There was no point in helping Wood, only to find he had to share cells with a dodgy inmate now Jason Smith was lying in the hospital, or he had to work with the wrong people. With Les's help, Tom had arranged for a slight re-shuffling to the cell allocation on the induction wing, and for a trusted inmate to look after him in the laundry. He hoped it was worth getting help for the lad as it had proved to be a costly enterprise, clearing both he and Shortie

93

out of all their reserves of tobacco. For the first time in twenty years Tom had a vested interest in another prisoner and he expected to have a good return on his investment.

Chapter 9

On Thursday afternoon, an hour before Nick was due to see his mother and sister, he collected his towel and went down to the ground floor, where the shower room was located at the back of the guard's office. Each inmate was allowed two showers a week in Blackthorpe. Normally one was taken the day of a visit. There was nothing more worrying for a wife or parent to see an inmate in a dirty and dishevelled state and every prisoner tried to look their best.

All three showers were in use when he entered the room and he stood quietly in the queue. He couldn't wait to get under the shower for a good soaking. The morning's work in the laundry had left him hot and sticky. Unusually the supervisor had decided to keep Nick working in the same department, even though there had been trouble there, but now he had a new work mate. His name was Lloyd Roberts and he was doing a ten stretch for armed robbery. He was a small man with a good sense of humour and an infectious laugh, but Nick had no doubt he was also pretty tough.

Nick had warmed to him immediately and felt lucky to be working alongside someone who appeared to be a decent bloke. But even with Lloyd entertaining him, time hung heavy that morning. Not only was he still worried about Jason, but with his friend injured on the hospital wing, he was worried another inmate like Scarface might be moved into his cell.

Slowly the shower queue became shorter and it wasn't long before Nick was able to wash off the dirt of the last few days. Jason had nicked his soap so he used the soap that was left on a small, dirty looking ledge next to the tap, trying not to think how many men had used it before him. Prison, Nick already realised, was not a place to be squeamish. He also tried to wash his hair with it, but soon found it was doing more harm than good. After towelling down he felt clean for the first time in days.

Nick's visit was booked for two o'clock and there was no need for him to go back to work. He had been told to remain in the cell until called and he lay on his bunk and tried to relax. He wondered how he would get on with his mum and hoped she wouldn't have a go at him. He also wondered if he would see his picture displayed on the walls. He had enjoyed painting the landscape but the next one would have to be different. He couldn't keep churning out the same thing and while he waited for his visit, he turned over the problem of what he could try next.

Nothing to do with prison, he thought. He found his mind drifting back over the years to when he was a kid and used to go fishing. Not far from his house, tucked away in a field behind the industrial estate, there was an old barn that belonged to the local farmer. He had often sheltered in it from the rain with his mates. Picturing it in his mind Nick could almost smell the damp hay that used to lie on the floor and the wooden beams that propped up its roof. My next picture, he decided. A combination of bold strokes and an increasing degree of fine detail. He had been told that practice makes perfect. It looked as though he was going to find out if that was true.

It was twenty past two when the guard opened the cell door and announced it was time to go. For a while Nick had thought the visit had been cancelled.

Those twenty minutes had seemed to last a life time. As he was escorted downstairs, he started to feel very nervous at the prospect of seeing his mum and sister. He had tried to look his smartest, clean shirt, jeans and socks, but his hair was in a right mess. It had become so matted, after washing it with prison soap, it felt to Nick as if he was wearing a wig made out of wire.

When Nick finally entered the visiting hall, the first thing he noticed was how it shined. The floor had been swept, unlike the others Nick had seen so far, and the tables and chairs looked as though they had been freshly washed down. There was a strange smell in the air and he couldn't figure out what it was. Then he realised it was disinfectant.

There were already a number of inmates sitting down busily talking to their visitors, and Nick was ordered to table number twenty-two. At first he couldn't find it and after quickly looking around the room there was also no sign of his mum or sister. He could feel himself starting to panic—*don't say they're not here!* He walked slowly up the room looking round until he saw them tucked away behind a pillar. A rush of emotion flooded through him as he walked towards the table. His mother stood up when she saw him but her smile quickly clouded over and was replaced by a look of concern. She took a pace towards her son and held out her arms. Nick gave his mum a hug and whispered. 'Thanks for coming.'

'No physical contact except holding hands!' boomed one of the guards.

Lisa pulled out a chair and told them both to sit down. Nick smiled at his sister and did as he was told. 'We were searched on the way in,' she told him quite unconcerned. 'Were they looking for drugs?'

His mother had considered it more of an ordeal. 'Made me feel like a criminal,' she said in disgust. 'Is it really necessary?' Nick nodded towards the CCTV cameras that were placed at strategic angles around the room. He told them what he had just learned himself—that most of the drugs were smuggled into prison during the visits and that's why the security had to be so tight.

For a while they sat and chatted about prison life in general, but Nick avoided talking about the danger on the wings. 'At least it's a clean prison,' said his mum glancing round the room. Nick nodded. He decided that it was better to let her believe that the rest of the prison was like the hall they were sitting in. He didn't want to tell her how dirty the rest of the place was, she'd already got enough to worry about. She asked him if he was eating enough. 'You're looking scrawny, Nick,' she said. Nick felt his stomach. 'I'm not that bad, just lost a pound or two.'

'There's a refreshment bar over there,' said his mum pointing to an alcove where volunteers were serving food. 'Can I get you something?'

Nick grinned. 'A cup of tea, a sandwich and a packet of cheese and onion crisps would be great.'

His mother took some money from her purse and Lisa, seeing it as an excuse to wander round, offered to go and get it. 'Anything else, while I'm at it?' she asked him.

'A Snickers bar? He turned to his mum. 'Is that all right, mum?' His mum smiled. 'Of course it is son, have whatever you want.'

They watched Lisa walking self-consciously across the room. Nick noticed that his sister had a decent pair of legs, and then he saw that he wasn't the only one to notice. An inmate was staring at her and it gave Nick an uneasy feeling. He'd like to tell his sister to wear jeans instead of a skirt on a future visit, but knew that if he said that, she'd probably turn up next time in something even shorter.

While Nick kept a watchful eye over his sister, he took the chance to glance round the hall. He scanned the walls to see if his picture was anywhere to be seen. On the wall next to him he spotted one he'd seen before in the art room, and there were some others hanging at the far end of the room, but worryingly there seemed nothing as colourful as his. *It can't have gone already,* he thought, at the same time as hoping it had.

'So, what else have you got to tell me,' asked his mother.

Nick turned to look at her. 'Nothing much, how about you. Any news?'

'Your father called,' she said.

'He came to see you?' asked Nick surprised.

'Don't be silly. He couldn't find the time, he phoned. He said he felt sick when he heard you'd been sentenced. He sends you his love. Says he's going to write.'

Nick pulled a petulant face. 'Huh—he needn't bother.' He wanted to change the subject. 'Mum, I've been given the chance to paint,' he said knowing how keen his mum had always been for him to take up painting for a living.

His mum's eyes lit up. 'That's marvellous,' she said thinking that there might be a positive side to this awful situation after all. Nick didn't add that he'd been forced into the situation.

Lisa returned with a full tray. 'You didn't give me enough money, mum, you owe me 60p.' Mrs Wood fumbled in her purse and handed Lisa a pound coin. Lisa took it saying that she was broke. Nick watched the financial transaction, embarrassed. He knew they must be struggling at home without the weekly contribution he'd been able to make from his grant. He suddenly felt guilty at having asked for so much to eat but when he opened the sandwich packet and took a bite he was glad he had. 'Hmm,' he said tasting the fresh bread. 'Real food.'

Whilst he was eating, he took another chance to look round the room, this time at some of the tables to see if any of the visitors had his picture, but again he could see nothing. 'Have you seen anyone looking at the pictures on the walls since you came in?' he asked his mother between mouthfuls.

'No dear,' she said. 'I don't think so.' Nick looked across at Lisa who shook her head.

He looked round again but this time an inmate sitting near him met his eyes and gave him a cold stare, bringing Nick quickly back down to earth and the stark reality of prison life. He returned his eyes to his own table realising that it wasn't wise, even if accidentally, to invade another prisoner's space. For the rest of the visit he continued to hide the truth from his mum about how bad it was inside. 'It's not too dangerous, I'm quite safe you know,' he said. He made them laugh by telling them edited highlights of the 'bang-up'. 'You should have heard it Lisa—rap, reggae, Coldplay.'

'Finish your visits,' shouted a guard from across the room. Nick thought the guard must have made a mistake. He was astounded that their forty minutes was up. Forty minutes at work seemed to drag forever but the visit was over in a flash. He was glad though that there was no time for long goodbyes as it would get too heavy. He gave his mum a peck on the cheek. 'Will you come again?' he asked them. Both his sister and mum nodded. 'Of course,' said his mum. 'Promise me you'll take care,' she said with a concerned look on her face.

'Relax mum,' said Nick forcing himself to smile. 'Nothing's going to happen to me.'

In a special holding cell located between the visiting hall and the rest of the prison, Nick's feeling of contentment was replaced with one of resignation, as he waited patiently to be searched before being allowed back to his wing. The guards were looking for drugs. Normally the packages of smack and dope, brought in by the visitors, were immediately swallowed by the inmates and were therefore undetectable. In the special cell, the prisoners had to undergo the humility of a strip search.

While Nick was waiting, he sat on a nearby bench and let himself reflect on the afternoon. The visit had been a bitter-sweet experience for him. Seeing his mother and sister again was a real tonic but on the other hand, it also evoked memories of happier times that Nick had now blown. He knew that some prisoners never had visits because they couldn't take the heart ache of saying goodbye each time, but on balance Nick decided the positive far outweighed the negative. Although the next visit would not be for two weeks, he was already looking forward to it. Nick had been told during his induction lecture that remaining in close contact with home was the most important ingredient for successful rehabilitation. Nick now understood why. He felt so good seeing his mum and sister, knowing they were supporting him, there was no way he would ever let his family down again.

After a brisk search Nick was told he could go back to the wing unescorted. Although his mind had been temporarily distracted away from thinking about his painting, the thought of what the Dragon might do to him if he couldn't raise the money, came crashing back with a vengeance and he was desperate to find out if his picture had sold. His journey took him close to the education block, and although he knew Amy was away, he couldn't help but look towards the art room to see if any lights were on. But there was no sign of life and he knew he would have to wait another agonising twenty four hours before finding out what had happened to his painting.

As he wandered along the corridor towards his wing, Nick noticed the lights were on in the medical centre and the door was open. The supervisor at work had told Nick that Jason had had twenty stitches in his chin, a badly broken jaw, four cracked ribs and a bust arm. With the seriousness of those injuries Nick had assumed that Jason would remain in an outside hospital for several days, but unbelievably, the supervisor had told him that Jason had been patched up and sent back to Blackthorpe within hours.

'Too expensive for the guards to watch over prisoners in hospital, so they're sent back as soon as possible. You'd have to be dead before they'd trust you not to make a run for it.' Deciding that he couldn't get into any trouble with the guards if he was in the medical centre, he decided to take a chance and ask the doctor if he could visit Jason.

The doctor was sitting at a desk filling out forms, when Nick knocked and walked into the surgery. 'Excuse me, Guv... I've come to see if I can visit Jason Smith, the man who got injured yesterday.

The doctor put down his pen and looked up. 'Are you talking about the young man that was beaten up?'

"Yes Guv.'

'And you are?'

'Wood 582... I found him Guv... I'm his cell mate, we're friends.'

The doctor looked at him closely. 'He's in a bad way, did you know that?'

'So I've been told, Guv,' he said nodding.

'Please stop calling me Guv—I'm a doctor, not one of the screws.'

'Sorry Gu..., doctor.' The doctor got up from the desk and walked towards an inner door. He was well aware of prison rules and knew that it was against regulations for inmates, who were not injured, to visit the hospital ward in the afternoon, but Smith was in a bad way and it would be good for him to see a friendly face.

'This way,' he said. 'You can see him for ten minutes, but only because it's the last chance you'll get.'

'He isn't dying is he?' asked Nick with a worried look on his face.

'No, they're moving him to another prison tomorrow.'

'*Tomorrow*?' said Nick aghast. 'Where to?'

'A place where they can look at his jaw properly. He'll be transferred from there when he's been treated, but goodness knows where to. Could be Scotland what with all the overcrowding.'

Nick was at a loss for words. A move that far away would mean no visits and Jason had told him that his Gran sometimes came to Blackthorpe. He'd said that she was the only relative that bothered about him. He'd told Nick that she had a heart condition and only managed to visit because she lived so near. 'Reckon she only does it 'cos there's no-one else to come and see me,' he'd said to Nick.

After seeing the pleasure on his mother's face that afternoon, Nick guessed that the visits would mean as much to the Gran as they did to Jason. He couldn't bear to think what it must be like not to have someone visit, or to have a loved one locked away.

The doctor took a key out of his pocket, slid it in the lock and within moments the heavy steel door that led to the ward was open. They had to pass through two more before they entered the sanctuary of the ward itself. Even though it was the hospital, security was still unrelenting. The windows were secured with heavy metal bars and the walls were thick enough to deter any form of escape plan. The ward room itself was eerily silent. There were six beds in total, three on either side and four out of the six were currently vacant. There was an old man with white hair in the middle bed on the right and he was clearly unwell. A hacking cough distorted his features but his mournful dark eyes never left Nick as he passed. Nick smiled sympathetically and moved on towards the end bed on the opposite side.

The sides of the bed had bars across to stop any patient falling out. Nick peered over and could just about make out it was Jason lying there by the one good eye. His friend was heavily bandaged across his chest and his head. Nick tried a smile but the groan he received back was a clear indication that Jason was still in great pain.

'Ten minutes then,' said the doctor turning away and walking towards the door.

Nick turned back to his friend. 'Thought you'd like some company,' he said not knowing if he'd made the right decision by coming. 'I hear you're being moved.'

Jason blinked a couple of times. Nick didn't really know what to say so he just rambled on, telling Jason that he hoped he had sold his painting, and that he had forgotten how good a Snickers bar tastes. He tried to sound jolly, but it wasn't a happy time. It struck Nick that he'd never visited a hospital before and as he looked down at his friend he hoped he wouldn't have to visit another for a very long time. Finally, Nick said it was time to go. It was then that Jason slowly raised his arm and pointed towards the far wall. Nick looked round, but all he could see were Jason's clothes lying on a chair.

'You want your clothes?' Nick asked. Jason nodded slowly. Nick went over and collected Jason's jeans and shirt. He took them back and placed them within reaching distance on the bed. Tentatively

Jason lifted his arm, took hold of his jeans and dug something out of the pockets. It was the sketch that Nick had drawn of his friend. Jason held it out. 'You want me to have this?' asked Nick. Jason nodded and Nick took the piece of paper, just as the door swung open and the doctor walked in.

Nick looked down at his friend. 'Time for me to go,' he said. Then a thought struck him. 'Write and let me know where you end up and I'll send you a letter,' he said enthusiastically. The reaction however was not what he expected. A tear welled up in his friend's eye, but Jason didn't turn away with embarrassment or try to hide in anyway, he just stared back at Nick and then slowly shook his head. 'You don't want to write?' said Nick flabbergasted.

'Come on, Wood' said the doctor walking towards him. Nick turned round to see the doctor beckoning. He nodded, then turned back for one last look at his friend. He tried to smile but he was feeling very let down. Even though he'd only known Jason a short time, a couple of weeks in prison can seem like a lifetime and Jason had become his friend and ally. He'd survived most things up to that point but this rejection was the final straw. *Why didn't his friend want to write? At least they could keep in touch.* If they didn't this was the end. They might never see each other again. He only had one friend in prison and now he wasn't going to have any. He stood looking down at Jason feeling more alone than ever. As he turned to leave, it was only to himself that he mumbled the words, 'Good luck Jason.'

The doctor had seen what had happened between the two young men and felt sorry for Wood. It was hard enough surviving the rigors of prison, without being on the end of a needless misunderstanding. 'Don't be too upset,' he said, as he led Nick to the entrance door. 'It's not that he doesn't want to keep in touch, he just can't.'

Nick didn't understand "What do you mean?" he asked.

The simplicity of the doctor's answer hammered home. 'He can't read or write,' he said.

Chapter 10

There was something wrong with the man on the floor. He could see blood coming from his head. He wanted to help but he couldn't. A dog was there in the shadows watching him, ready to attack if he made the smallest move. He could hear it growling. Suddenly the dog was coming at him fast. He tried to run, but couldn't run fast enough. He fell, and the dog was on him, snarling, mouth open, gums back, teeth bared. Blood and saliva dropped from its open mouth and fell onto his face.

Nick woke up spluttering and spitting. He put his hand to his mouth and tried to wipe away the blood, but there was none there, just drops of water. *'Drops of water,'* he said to himself as he came awake. Then he looked up towards the window and saw that rain was being blown in through the small crack. It was hammering down outside. He huddled himself beneath his blanket and rolled up tightly against the wall. He'd had a terrible night. Being on his own for the first time hadn't been fun and he realised how comforting it had been, having Jason in his cell at night. No new inmate had materialised yet and being banged up alone was no joke.

His mind had been so mixed up that he'd stayed awake most of the night in turmoil, and his problems were still there as daylight came into the cell. It seemed they were always going to be there, or at least while he was in prison.

The night before, he hadn't felt like doing anything when he'd returned after tea. Seeing Jason had upset him. He couldn't face looking at the picture he had drawn of his friend, so he'd put it in a small box where he kept his other sketches. He'd just sat and thought for a while, contemplating what would happen to him if his painting hadn't sold. It was the fear of what might happen to him in the future, that had driven him to start his next picture. He couldn't afford the luxury of waiting to see if anyone had bought it. He had to start the next one straight away.

He had concentrated for several hours. It was much more complicated working on the fine detail of the barn than on his field of flowers, and he'd progressed painstakingly slowly. He had left the painting on the table before going to bed, as he didn't want it drying out too quickly.

When Nick became fully awake, he lent across and glanced at his previous night's efforts. The sight of the old barn evoked powerful memories of his youth and not for the first time, Nick regretted having picked such an emotional subject. For the first time in a long while, Nick had had nightmares.

Fortunately Lloyd, his workmate, was in good humour that morning and time passed relatively quickly in the laundry, until the hooter sounded at lunch, signifying the end of the week. There was no work on Friday afternoons and before clocking off, each inmate was given a pay slip, showing how much had been transferred into their accounts. Before leaving the laundry, Nick quietly took his into a corner, nervously opened the envelope and looked at the slip, hoping for a full week's wage of seven pounds.' When he read the words his heart missed a beat: Three pounds. *Three pounds,* he said to himself in complete shock. He then read the words printed below the amount. Four pounds had been deducted for the sessions he'd missed; the governor's interview and his visit. He couldn't believe it. *This is fucking ridiculous,* he thought.

He'd been feeling more confident of being able to pay off the Dragon, now he wasn't so sure. And he wouldn't be finding out until later in the day, *and by then it might be too late.* Three pounds would only allow him to buy one phone card and stupidly, he had used the one he'd been given to call Jessica. Now his only hope lay in his picture being sold. Nick tried to remain calm. He told himself it was now out of his hands, as there was little else he could do, but his imagination was taking off, and all he could think about was which bed he would occupy in the medical centre, if everything went wrong at canteen that night.

* * *

Just as Nick was finding out about his pay packet, two guards lay in wait at the entrance to the lifer's wing. They were waiting for one of the lifers to return from work. They had been given some information from the governor which they decided must have come from the grass. The governor was eager for another conviction. When the first batch of prisoners appeared they were allowed to pass through onto the wing, but when Charlie Baxter and Shortie sauntered in, the guards moved forward. 'Don't move Baxter,' one of them said.

He walked up to Charlie. 'Arms in the air Baxter—legs apart!'

Shortie looked on in amazement, *What the hell is this all about*? he wondered, but it wasn't long before he found out. Charlie was given a rub down search: first his arms then down the sides of his chest, and then his legs. It was there the guard felt the bottle of hooch. 'Found it,' he said.

'Let's see what you're smuggling in shall we Baxter? Get it out,' said the other officer holding out his hand.

Charlie went white. He reached into his overalls and took out the bottle of booze he'd only bought minutes before and handed it to the screw. He felt sick. He was soon expecting a move to a better prison and this would definitely count against him. It was the first time in two years he had thought of having a drink. *How the hell did they know?* he thought.

The officers ordered him upstairs and told him to wait in his cell until further notice. Charlie walked along the corridor in a daze, wondering what would happen to him. He'd spent the last fifteen years keeping his nose clean and now this. Shortie looked at Charlie's white face as they climbed the stairs. There was little he could say to his friend to make him feel better. He patted his back in sympathy when Charlie turned off on the second landing, and for a moment Shortie stared after him, shaking his head in disbelief. He then carried on up to the top of the stairs, but instead of going directly to his cell he walked to the end of the landing, where he knew Tom was likely to be. He knocked and entered to find his friend sitting on his bed. 'We've got a problem,' he said to Tom. 'The grass has just nailed Charlie.'

* * *

On Friday afternoons, if it wasn't raining, the exercise yard was open for the prisoners to walk round or have a kick about if they could find a ball. Not wanting to stay in his cell, Nick decided to venture out into the fresh air. On his journey to work each day, he walked across the yard, but he had never been out to see it when it had been open for exercise. It was covered in tarmac and about the size of a five-a-side football pitch. Lines were drawn on the ground and goal posts marked at each end. Within minutes a football match was taking place. Those not taking part, sauntered clockwise round the outside edge. Nick joined the line, slotting in behind two inmates who were busy talking to one another. They weren't talking quietly and it was easy for Nick to overhear their conversation.

'See up there, Des,' said one of the men pointing. 'That's the lifer's wing. One of them has done nearly twenty-two years.'

'*Twenty-two years*?' exclaimed Des. 'Jesus! Anyone who's done that amount of bird's got to be off their rocker.' Nick didn't say so, but he totally agreed. He'd hardly spent any time in prison and already he felt half mad. *God knows what I'd be like after two decades,* he thought. He pulled his collar up and stuffed his hands into his pockets, feeling cold all of a sudden. Before Jason had got himself beaten up he'd told Nick what he knew about the lifers at Blackthorpe, apparently there were about thirty. They didn't mix with the other prisoners as they preferred to keep themselves to themselves. The only time they could be seen with other inmates was at work in the metal shop. They even had their own canteen.

'Scarface told me they're dangerous,' he'd told Jason. 'They'd cut your throat as soon as look at yer.'

'Look at it this way,' Jason had said shrugging. 'If I was starting a thirty stretch and some bastard screw told me to do something I didn't want to, I wouldn't hesitate to 'muller' 'im. So what if you kill the geezer? You're already doin' life,' he'd said. The Dragon was bad enough, but the lifers sounded even worse. *God forbid I ever meet one* he thought, as he looked up at the tall, grey building that faced him.

* * *

From high up in the lifer's wing, Tom Hawks looked down at the exercise yard. Some of the prisoners had wandered outside for some fresh air. He watched a brawl break out amongst the ones playing football and thought, *thank God I don't have to mix with that rabble any more.*

He lent across to his radio and turned up the music a little. He'd recently started listening to classical music and his favourite piece on the CD was just about to come on. He was in a sad mood. He liked Charlie and now he might be knocked back for a few months. He closed his eyes and thought about the information that had been passed to him since his mates had been keeping their eyes and ears open. It was the only way they had a chance of catching the grass, but so far nothing useful had come up.

Apparently a kid called Spencer had bought some dope off the Dragon earlier that day and now owed a staggering twelve phone cards. *Won't be long before he has to visit the medical centre,* Tom thought. Two inmates, Gregory 425 and James 766 had stolen a side of ham from the kitchen that morning and the prison didn't even know it was missing yet. There were also rumours about the guards. Five consecutive Fridays, Mr Hodges had reported in sick, but he hadn't been at home in bed. He'd been moonlighting at the local builder's yard earning some quiet cash. And then there was the governor himself. Now there were plenty of rumours about the governor, but worryingly, none about the grass.

Tom opened his eyes and looked back at the scene below. Three men were looking up towards the lifer's wing. Squinting, Tom could make out that one of them was Wood 582. Tom grinned. Nick Wood had been lucky to escape the wrath of the governor when he had been interrogated about the Jason Smith incident. Getting Pete Vacanni involved had been a costly business. He was now shelling out tobacco to the inmate looking after Nick in the laundry and he also owed Dave Walker, a trusted mate who was not only going to share cells with the kid, he was also going to keep an eye him at canteen that night in case things kicked off. Not that the kid knew it. *He must be shittin' himself,* thought Tom. *Only time will tell if he's worth the effort.* But for the first time since arriving in HMP Blackthorpe, time wasn't on Tom's side. After spending so much time behind bars, Tom had a feel for prisons, and he knew this one was ready to explode.

* * *

The term 'canteen' can be confusing in prison. Not only does it refer to part of the kitchen where inmates collect and eat their food, it also refers to the time of the week when prisoners can spend their weekly wage. In HMP Blackthorpe 'canteen' took place every Friday night in the corridor between the doctor's surgery and the education department.

Normally the small hatchway would be seen as an inconspicuous hole in the wall. On Friday nights the hatchway was opened outwards to the waiting inmates and it became the focal point of the prison. Inside, two guards kept the hoards out and protected the paymaster from getting lynched. There was meant to be a queue outside but it always turned into a writhing mass of bodies, like bees round a honey pot. Nick couldn't believe the scene when he entered the corridor. It reminded him of the news shots he'd seen on television about the stock exchanges, where hundreds of men shouted at each other, frantically waving around pieces of paper in what seemed complete chaos.

Nick blanched at the thought of having to make his way through the throng on his own, but suddenly an inmate was walking alongside him. Nick had never seen him before. 'There used to be a guard overlooking the queue, but it became so dangerous for him they now let us fend for ourselves,' the inmate shouted. 'Stick close to me or you'll end up with nothing.'

Nick wasn't sure what to make of his escort, but looking at the mass of bodies fighting to get serve, he was glad of the support. Every time Nick was bumped or jostled, and in danger of being knocked to the ground, he was grabbed by the stranger. Nick started to wonder if he was gay, but the man seemed totally unconcerned with him unless he needed help.

There were only a few men in the whole corridor not involved in the melee. They stood away from the crowd, near the exit door, collecting their weekly dues. Nick felt sick at the sight of the Dragon, who stood majestically amongst his henchmen, smiling like the cat that'd got the cream. Nick hated the man, but after worrying so much about his safety, he was also starting to hate the prison officers who allowed the bullying to take place.

Eventually Nick managed to squeeze his way to the front of the queue and gave his name to the paymaster. One of the guards confirmed his identity and then signalled for him to place his order. It took a few moments for him to compose himself, but he had to ask quickly as so many inmates were pressing to get close.

'How much have I got to spend Guv?' he shouted. *Please be enough* he thought to himself while his account was checked. The Paymaster looked down his list and Nick took the chance to glance towards the end of the corridor. If he didn't have enough cash, his only chance would be to try to run the opposite way from the Dragon and beg sanctuary in the doctor's office.

'Eight pounds,' said the paymaster jogging Nick's mind back from planning his escape.

'Eight pounds,' he repeated loudly knowing instantly that someone had bought his painting. *'Eight bloody pounds'*. Suddenly all his pent up worry evaporated, he thumped the counter in delight. He was going to be safe for one week at least. 'Well, what do you want?" asked the Paymaster impatiently.

Nick wished he could bottle up the relief he felt and flog it behind the counter. He could see all sorts of things, from sweets and packets of crisps, to shampoo and toothpaste, but in the back of his mind he wondered if he would ever manage to sell another picture and decided to buy the minimum. Nick felt his anger rise as he turned down the temptation of food. He was desperate for something nice to eat but he couldn't take the risk. 'Just two phone cards please, Guv,' he said. The paymaster gave them to Nick at the same time as shouting, 'Next!'

An inmate quickly shoved Nick out of the way and he was on the point of stumbling when someone grabbed him by the collar and yanked him upright. Nick held the phone cards in the palm of his hand as though his life depended on it. He realised, with a sick feeling in his stomach, that that was probably the case. He followed a path cut through the surging crowd by the stranger, but when he emerged the man had miraculously disappeared. Nick walked to the end of the corridor. Four burly inmates stood with the Dragon. The Weasle stood to one side. 'You've come to pay,' said the man who had made his life hell.

Nick didn't answer the Dragon, he just handed over the cards.

'Next week, same time, same place, eh Wood. Don't forget, there's a good lad.' Nick heard the Dragon laughing as he turned his back and retreated down the corridor. As he walked back to his wing, the prospect of having to pay the Dragon every week hit him hard. He'd been in prison only two weeks but it felt like a lifetime. Months and months stretched ahead of him, pressure every week. *How the hell am I going to get through this?* he asked himself.

Chapter 11

There is little consistency in prison; the rules change from day to day. New prisoners come into jail every week and men who have served their time are released. Even cellmates change. Hardly anything remains constant, especially not emotions. During his first two weeks in prison, Nick had travelled the full emotional spectrum. He could have been excused for thinking that things might calm down, but over the next few months he swayed back and forth from sadness to happiness, in a flux that was driven by chaos. The only emotion that remained constant was fear.

Throughout summer Nick painted feverishly and never missed a payment to the Dragon. Several times he thought he would. Twice he'd been so ill that he hadn't been able to work at all and he'd relied on his savings. Every week he tried to complete another picture to top up his meagre account. Three times he had completed his work at the last minute and the paintings were still damp when he'd handed them over to Amy. Miraculously they were all sold—but the pressure had taken its' toll.

As summer came to an end, Nick's weight had dropped to eight stone. Two stone lighter than when he first came to Blackthorpe. His hair had grown long and his skin had become spotty. His mother and Lisa visited regularly, but at the end of their last visit, his mother had burst into tears. No longer could he could pretend all was well within the prison walls. They knew he must be suffering.

There was one aspect in Nick's life that gave him hope and that was his painting. Through necessity his skills had developed and by anybody's standards he had become an exceptional artist. So exceptional, that the head of the education department had created a new post for him to fill, that of art department orderly. Instead of working in the laundry, he now ventured to the art room every morning. His duties were simple. It was his job to prepare everything for the art classes that took place most afternoons. He cleaned the pallets, cut the paper into manageable sizes and made sure all the work tops were clean. When he had completed his tasks he was allowed to paint.

Very occasionally, if one of the staff were staying late, Nick would be allowed back into the room in the evening so he could take advantage of the bright electric lights rather than the dim light in his cell. On those occasions he would be given a key and told to lock himself inside the room. If he had to go out for any reason, even if he was just walking to the department office, no more than twenty yards away, he still had to lock up. There were valuable items in the art room that some inmates would pay dearly for. Solvents that helped clean the brushes were stored in the cupboards. A whole assortment of glues were kept in stock. Blocks of wax that could be used to create certain effects on paper were stashed underneath a work bench. All were perfectly innocent in the hands of an up and coming artist, but in the wrong hands they could be sold for profit: glue and solvents to the 'sniffers', wax to make candles for the heroin users. Consequently, at the end of each day all inmates were thoroughly searched before being allowed to return to the wing. The education staff trusted Nick. They knew he would never jeopardise the opportunity of working in the art room, but for his own protection he was thoroughly searched as well.

Late one afternoon after Nick had finished his duties in the art room, while he was waiting to be searched, he found himself looking out of the art department window. The leaves on the trees outside were starting to turn and Nick decided that soon he would paint the scene. Being given more time to paint had allowed him to take on quite detailed work. No longer did he have to manically work away at night in his cell. He could now take his time, and it had reaped rewards. His slow brush strokes were carried out with a steadiness of hand that would have made a surgeon jealous. Nick knew that if he had to be in prison, he couldn't have found a better place to be.

There were two things in particular that were helping Nick survive his time in prison. His new cell mate, and Amy. Incredibly the inmate he now shared with was the man who had looked after Nick during his first trip to the canteen.

'My name's Dave,' he'd said in greeting. 'I don't smoke—I don't do drugs and while you share with me, neither will you. Got it?' Dave was about fifty, Nick guessed and he'd obviously done a few years inside, but when Dave was around Nick always felt safe. The other aspect that made his life tolerable was working alongside Amy. There was no one who boosted his confidence more.

Just as Nick was thinking that he couldn't have hand picked better people to mix with, Amy entered the art room with a guard following behind. She hated subjecting him to the routine search but *'rules are rules,'* she said to herself with a sigh. She smiled when Nick turned round. He was well acquainted with the system. He walked over to the nearest work top and carefully turned out his trouser pockets. Then the guard gave him a rub down search to make sure nothing was concealed beneath his clothing. Nick took off his shoes and smiled at Amy as the guard inspected the soles.

'Open up,' said the guard as he looked in Nick's mouth to see if he was concealing anything under his tongue. 'Okay off you go.'

'See you tomorrow,' Nick said as he waved to Amy over his shoulder.

For the first time since arriving in prison, Nick almost felt happy. Being able to paint regularly had become an important part of his life, and not just because it enabled him to pay off his debts to the Dragon every week. Like most people, Nick enjoyed doing something that he was really good at, and for the first time *ever* he was getting real satisfaction from painting.

After tea that day Nick made his way along to the gym with his cell mate. Whilst he had become very thin, he'd actually become stronger. Although Dave was a man of few words he had virtually insisted on Nick training and three times a week they would go to the gym to lift weights.

The gym was like the village hall back in Nick's hometown. There was a badminton court that was constantly in use and the multi gym was always busy. Most of the time they would use the free weights that were stored around the edges of the walls. Nick nodded to several people he knew when he entered, including Lloyd, his former work mate. Although he no longer worked in the laundry, he had remained friends with Lloyd and they would often train together. Both Dave and Lloyd were phenomenally strong. The first time Nick had tried heaving up just half of what they could manage, he'd almost burst a blood vessel. So had Dave and Lloyd with laughter. 'You can't be that fuckin' weak,' Lloyd had said. Since then he'd become stronger and could now easily lift his body weight above his head.

Nick was just about to start his third set of bench presses that evening when an inmate tapped him on the shoulder. 'Screw on the wing wants to see you, Wood.'

Nick bent down, picked up a towel and wiped

the sweat off his face. 'What about?' he asked with a slight frown. The inmate shrugged his shoulders, turned round and wandered off.

Nick turned back to Dave. 'Gotta go back to the wing for a minute' he said throwing his sweaty towel onto the floor. Dave nodded, bent down and picked up more weight to put on the bench press bar. Nick made his way out of the gym, wondering what the wing officer could possibly want.

He was just passing the downstairs washroom on his way to the guard's office when the door burst open. Nick jumped in surprise but before he could react, trapped like a rabbit in headlights, two men grabbed him and dragged him roughly inside.

Nick couldn't believe it. W*hat the fuck's going on?* he thought, suddenly feeling vulnerable. It had been months since he had felt real gut churning fear and the emotion hit him full force. Two men shoved him roughly into the middle of the room and then stood behind him blocking the door. When Nick regained his balance he looked up and there, standing in front of him, was the Dragon. He was holding his hands out in an apologetic gesture. 'Only way we could have a private chat,' he said.

Nick thought about shouting out, but he wasn't in debt to the Dragon, what's more he had never missed a payment. Although he felt scared, he didn't think he was in any immediate danger.

'Times are hard, Wood,' said the Dragon, explaining the abduction. 'Lots of inmates to supply drugs to, not much gear comin' in.' Then his lips parted in an evil grin. 'How's the art department stores at the moment?'

Nick now understood what the Dragon wanted. He shook his head. 'Not a chance,' he said. This was one time Nick found it easy to say 'no'. Even if the Dragon threatened to beat him to pulp, there was no way he would betray the trust he had been shown by the education staff. There was absolutely no way he would betray Amy.

'Had a feeling you'd say that. Not quite the terrified little one you used to be, eh Wood.' Nick stood rooted to the spot. 'That gives me a big problem Nick. My customers 'ave seen you in that art room. They keep saying 'Get him to nick stuff', but of course we both know you won't. You won't cross that slag of an art teacher will you?' His eyes narrowed and the smile was replaced with a sneer.

Nick's anger boiled over and he made a move towards the Dragon, but iron hands quickly clamped onto his shoulders. The Dragon continued as Nick was held firm. 'Now I admire that Nick, I really do. No way I'd ever be loyal to a slag bitch like her, but that gives me a serious problem. I can't let the inmates think you can say 'no' to me and get away with it now can I? I've got to show them I'm still in control.' The Dragon took a pace towards Nick and a hand came from behind and clamped itself over his mouth. Nick started to struggle. Whatever was going to happen, it wasn't going to be pleasant and beads of sweat started to form on his forehead.

He could do nothing as the Dragon reached out, grabbed his right hand and pulled it forward. The Dragon then took hold of Nick's two middle fingers and slowly started to bend them back. All the time the Dragon looked Nick straight in the eye. 'We'll forget the payments for a while,' he said. 'You won't be doing any art for some time.'

Nick felt sick. He desperately tried to pull his arm back, but it was held firm. Sweat dripped to the ground. He tried to struggle but he couldn't. Then the tendons started to rip and he started to gag. Inside his head a voice screamed *'NO'*. Then sickeningly, he heard the bones snap.

* * *

About an hour after Nick's bones and tendons were ripped apart Tom Hawks sat in his cell on the lifer's wing staring at the wall. Six months before it had been bare. Now the most amazing pictures hung from it. The first one he had bought was his favourite, all that colour, but every one he had acquired since was special to him. Every Thursday for the last few months, he had eagerly waited for Amy to visit the lifer's wing and bring him the lad's latest work. He and the other lifers had bought them all, and framed them, except for one that Amy had bought herself.

Amy had spotted that young Wood had talent. Tom now knew it as well. If he practised for a hundred years he wouldn't be able to paint like the kid, but he hadn't let Amy tell Nick that his pictures never got as far as the visiting hall. For one thing the Dragon would find out and the price of protection would soar. But in a selfish way he needed the kid to be under pressure. Amy said Nick had improved enormously since he'd been painting regularly. Fear had made him better.

In all his time inside, Tom had never had such a rewarding time. Not only did he feel good about keeping Nick Wood safe, but he now felt like a real art collector. It was tough to remain sane when serving a life sentence, but his new-found interest made him feel like a person again. Insatiably he had read every art book Amy had lent him and the collection of Nick's work had become his most prized possession. It had also distracted Tom's mind away from the troubles in the rest of the prison. For weeks, during the spring, Tom and the other lifers had tried to find out who the grass was, but he remained undetected and now Tom had all but given up.

At least Tom didn't have to worry about Nick being safe on the wing. Dave Walker was doing a good job looking after the boy. At first Dave was paid half an ounce of burn every week to watch over Nick, but Dave now did it for nothing He liked and respected young Nick Wood, though he'd never let the lad know it.

Suddenly a knock on the door brought Tom out of his daydream and officer Les Wright poked his head round the corner. He knew Tom had really enjoyed the last few months and he regretted having to deliver the awful news about his protégé. Tom looked up and saw the worried expression on his face. 'What's happened Les?' he asked.

* * *

Nick woke up the next day in the hospital wing. A vicious throbbing pain enveloped his whole arm and he had a numbing headache. He looked down to where the pain was at its most excruciating and saw his hand was in plaster.

The doctor was standing to one side of his bed. 'Remember what happened?' he asked. Nick felt very groggy but he tried to clear his mind. Step by step he went through what he could recall, working out in the gym, being told to go back to the wing, *then being hauled into the washroom.* The events of the previous night came thundering back but Nick tried to hide his expression. 'No,' he said shaking his head and feeling sick with the pain.

'You've got concussion,' said the doctor. 'You must have banged your head on the floor when you passed out.' Gently the doctor picked up Nick's hand and inspected the plaster and bandages. 'Your two middle fingers have been snapped at the joint. We've reset them. Should be out of plaster in about six weeks.' He moved away from the bed. 'Governor's coming to see you later, I should get some rest if I were you.' It sounded to Nick as if the doctor wanted to add. 'You'll need it.'

Physically Nick felt terrible and mentally he

was still very groggy, but there were no gaps in his memory. *Pity,* he thought as once again he went over what had happened. He shut his eyes when he re-lived the blinding flash of pain.

Had Nick been able to think clearly, he might have fully understood the dilemma that faced him, but before he had time to regain full awareness the governor came to visit.

'How are you 582?' he asked in a crystal clear voice. His small head bent over Nick and he studied the patient through thin, narrow eyes.

'Okay, thank you Sir.'

'So who did this to you then?'

Nick hadn't given much thought to the interview. Just a case of keeping his mouth shut like the last time. 'I can't remember what happened sir.'

The governor turned round, pulled up a chair and sat down. 'I want you to try and remember,' he said. 'I want to stop this bullying.'

For a moment Nick was tempted to talk. It sounded as though the governor meant it, and Nick was fed up with the terror. He thought of Jason and all the others who'd suffered at the hands of the Dragon, but he needed time to think about the consequences of telling the truth and continued with the pretence. 'I can't remember Sir. It's all a blank,' he said letting a confused expression cross his face.

The governor sat back clearly trying not to show his irritation. He was thinking about the latest memo from the Home Office. There were apparently two question marks about his record. One was over the amount of inmates who were having 'accidents' at Blackthorpe. 'I fell down the stairs, Guv,' or 'I slipped outside playing football,' were reasons given to the doctor for the injuries, but it was suspected that bullying had caused many of them. The other blight on his record was the apparent lack of educational encouragement. Hardly any inmates studied anything at Blackthorpe. The governor had three months in which to turn round these apparent blips before the prison inspectors' visit, when his future could be decided.

The governor lent forward. 'If you can't remember what happened, I can't let you back in the prison,' he said dropping the bombshell on Nick. 'I have to assume that you were beaten up and that it will happen again. You'll have to be transferred. Problem is—I don't know where you'll end up. Do you remember your work mate Jason Smith?' he asked. Nick nodded slowly.

'Hundred and fifty miles away he is now,' continued the governor. 'Only prison with room. A real shame. No chance of his grandmother visiting of course.' The governor paused but then threw out the barely veiled threat. 'You have visits don't you 582?'

Nick's mother and sister had visited him regularly throughout the summer. Along with his enjoyment of painting, their visits had kept Nick from falling into the abyss of depression. The thought that he could be transferred to some God-forsaken prison miles from home appalled him. It would devastate his mum.

Nick realised he could no longer rely on his original story, that he simply couldn't remember. If he did he would be transferred. Yet he couldn't grass on the Dragon. The stigma attached to someone who was known as a grass would follow them right through the system. There would be no hiding. Eventually, one night in some distant washroom, they would receive punishment. The thought of having boiling water poured over him terrified Nick. He didn't know what to say and just looked blank faced at the governor.

'Almost heard the cogs turning 582,' the governor said standing up. 'I'll leave you with this little conundrum until later—think about it. It's your move next 582, but it had better be good.' The governor walked briskly out of the room, leaving Nick to stew on his own.

When the governor had disappeared, the doctor slipped quietly from behind a curtain where he had been secretly listening to the interrogation. His jaw was set with determination as he walked back into his office, where he took out a piece of notepaper from his desk. The doctor had his finger on the pulse of more than his sick inmates—he knew more about the internal workings of the prison than anyone else.

The governor didn't care about the welfare of the inmates, he was too preoccupied manipulating the statistics that went to the Home Office, saying how efficiently the prison was being run.

One thing that grated on the doctor more than anything was the bullying. He was fed up with having to stitch up young inmates who were being subjected to intolerable punishment. There were many rumours as to who was responsible, but every time a newly bashed up youngster found his way to the hospital ward, the fear of being labelled a grass would keep them quiet—but their silence was rewarded with a transfer. Too many young men had suffered needlessly in Blackthorpe and he wasn't about to see it happen again. The doctor wrote a note on the paper then folded up the sheet and stuffed it inside an empty bottle of pills.

Chapter 12

Tom Hawks was getting ready for work when there was a knock at the door and Shortie walked in holding a paper bag in his hand that he had just collected from the medical centre. He handed it to Tom who opened the bag and took out a small bottle of pills.

He unscrewed the top and took out the piece of paper, unfolded it and then read the note. Sure enough the governor had been to see young Wood. When Tom had digested the words he tore the paper into small pieces and threw them away. He glanced round at Shortie. 'Time to act,' he said.

There was only one person who could possibly help. Purposefully he walked out of the cell, along the corridor and climbed down the stairs to the guards' office. Three guards sat inside. They looked up as Tom entered. 'I need to go to the education department,' he said.

Amy looked up when Tom knocked and entered the art room. Over the last few months she had come to know Tom as well as any other prisoner and she immediately knew something was wrong. 'What's the matter?' she asked.

Tom looked round at the guard who had escorted him. 'It's all right officer,' said Amy guessing that Tom wanted to talk to her on his own. 'I need Hawks to help me for a while. I'll call the wing when I've finished with him.' The guard nodded and wandered off.

Tom then told Amy the news. 'Nick's in the medical centre. He had his fingers broken last night'.

"*What?*" she said, aghast.

'The governor's just been to see him. He told him unless he names his attacker he'll be shipped out.'

'Do you think he will?' she asked, looking visibly shaken.

'And be labelled a grass? No chance. If he's learned one thing in prison it'll be to keep his mouth shut. Unless we do something he'll be gone within

125

days.'

'Oh no Tom, that'll destroy him. Isn't there anything we can do?'

Tom looked back towards the door to make sure no one outside was listening. 'The only way is a plea from you lot up here. You know how proud the governor is of his prison record. Well, rumour has it that that he needs to pull his socks up. Tell him Nick's a main contender for the National Prison Education awards. It might make a difference.'

Amy thought for a minute. Nick was certainly good enough. But even if she managed to persuade the governor that Nick *should* stay, there was another problem. 'Where could they put him?' she asked, knowing Nick wouldn't be allowed to go back to his wing if he maintained he couldn't remember what happened. And if he told the truth, he'd be transferred. No grass could stay. It was catch-22. It seemed no matter what he did, there was no place in Blackthorpe for young Nick Wood.

'There's only one way to get him out of this. Tell the governor there's a spare cell on the lifer's wing,' said Tom. 'Tell him we'll look after him.'

'He'll *never* buy that Tom,' she said shaking her head.

'Well I don't reckon he's got much option. The doctor's willing to back us up and say he's got amnesia. He'll say Nick's too concussed to travel and that he's bound to remember soon. It'll be too tempting for him. He'll have a shot at the kid winning an award for the prison *and* when Nick regains his memory he might also be able to convict the bully. Believe me, Amy,' said Tom. 'It's the only way to keep him here.' Amy pondered the logic and her mind was quickly made up. 'When should I see the governor, Tom.'

A look of relief swept over Tom's face. With Amy supporting him there was a chance his plan might work. 'No time like the present,' he said.

* * *

Just before lunch that day, the governor returned to the hospital ward. He'd just spent half an hour with Amy Jones from the art department, who had offered him an interesting solution to his problem. After being let into the ward by the doctor, he found young Wood lying in the same position he'd been in at their last meeting, but on his face was a different expression: one of resignation. 'Well 582, recovered your memory?' he asked.

Having had time to think things through, Nick had resigned himself to keeping his mouth shut and spending his remaining time in prison far away from home. He couldn't grass on the Dragon. 'No sir,' he said with finality.

The governor paused. 'I've been told that memories return given time 582, and I'm going to give you that time,' he said. 'But you can't stay in here, and I can't take the risk of putting you back on the wing.' The governor's face took on an unusual expression. 'Until your memory returns, there's only one place you can go—the spare cell on the lifer's wing.'

Even though he was still groggy, the impact of what the governor was saying hit him full force and his blood froze in his veins.

'You'll move at dawn tomorrow 582, before the prison comes to life. We'll talk again in a couple of days, when perhaps your memory has returned. Until then happy dreams.' The governor swept out of the room before Nick had a chance to plead. Everything had been going so much better for him, but now his life seemed all but over. The lifers were the most dreaded of all prisoners and now Nick was to be locked up with them. He cringed as Scarface's words came back to haunt him. *They'd cut your throat as soon as look at yer.*

That night Nick hardly slept a wink. His mind was reeling from what the governor had said. Living with lifers had to be the worst form of torture and he was moving to their lair in a few hours. Eventually he drifted off to sleep, but twice he woke up shouting.

When he was woken in the morning, the doctor helped him get ready and dressed his arm in a sling. Nick tried everything he could to delay the inevitable, but shortly before dawn a guard came into the doctor's office carrying Nick's bag of personal possessions from his old cell. He was there to escort Nick to his new home. 'See you again soon,' said the doctor, as the guard led him into the deserted corridor.

All too soon probably, thought Nick. He felt sick. His hand still throbbed and a pain hammered away in the back of his head. But it was nothing to the pain he thought might be inflicted on him shortly.

The doctor watched the young man go and then sat down at his desk. A hint of a smile was on his lips. He had enjoyed helping Tom Hawks. He'd known him for two years, ever since he'd first come to Blackthorpe, and in that time he'd come to like and respect the lifer, as much as he loathed and mistrusted the governor.

Too many times he'd watched the system grind inmates to their knees. This time he had acted and taken a big risk. Not only had he lied to the governor about the state of Nick's concussion, but he'd also sent confidential information to an inmate. If he was ever found out, it would mean a severe reprimand, probably the sack. The small smile broke into a fully fledged one however, when he realised the risk was worth it. For once, one of the young inmates might be saved.

* * *

When the guard reached the entrance door to the lifer's wing he kicked it hard, informing those inside that they had arrived. From inside Nick could hear the jangling of keys and moments later the door swung open. A huge guard stepped forward and signalled for Nick to enter. For a moment he hesitated, hoping that there might be a last-minute reprieve, but the guard behind guided him forward, dropped his bag on the floor and moments later he heard the heavy iron door slam shut.

'Well, well, the famous Wood 582,' said the guard in deep bass voice. 'Happy about being here?' he asked, grinning.

This one's a right sadist, thought Nick. He didn't recognise the man. At one time or another he'd seen most of the guards in the prison. This one, Nick guessed, was permanently stationed with the lifers. *Probably off his rocker, like the rest of them here.*

The big man picked up the bag off the floor, turned his back on Nick and headed for the stairs. 'You're on the third floor, right at the top. Nice view from the window,' he said.

Great, Nick thought all the further to fall from.

It was still very early in the morning and there were no lifers around, they were all still asleep, but Nick dreaded to think what it would be like later. He was so pre-occupied contemplating the danger he faced, he didn't notice that the stairs were sparkling clean.

When they reached his new cell on the top floor, the guard pulled open the door and slung his bag on top of the only bed. It wasn't a bunk bed as he had been used to. 'Aren't I sharing Guv? he asked.

The guard looked surprised. 'Do you want to?'

'*No,*' Nick blurted out.

'Right then,' said the guard. 'It's still early, so I suggest you lie down for a while. Someone will be up to see you later.' With that, he turned on his heels and went out leaving the door ajar. Nick rushed out. 'Guv,' he called out in a loud whisper. 'Aren't you going to lock the door?'

'You'll be all right,' he said. 'Don't panic.'

Nick looked along the landing. To his horror he saw that none of the doors were locked. Quietly he made his way back inside the cell, pulled the bed away from the wall with his good hand, and pushed it up against the door. It would give him those few necessary seconds in which to scream for help. He also slipped his arm out of the sling the doctor had given him. He needed to be ready for action. With little else to do, Nick lay down on the bed and waited until the morning bell sounded, when the wing would come to life and he could expect the first attack.

* * *

Tom Hawks looked at the watch he was allowed to keep in his cell. It was early, but he knew the new addition to the lifer's wing would now be alone in his cell. He swung his legs over the side of the bed, yawned and stretched his arms above his head. He collected his wash kit off the window ledge and walked out of his unlocked cell to the washroom.

'Morning, Shortie,' he said, greeting his friend who was already shaving. The window in the washroom was open and the air inside was clean and fresh.

Tom stripped to the waist and splashed cold water on to himself. He then meticulously shaved. Finally, while humming a Beatles song to himself, he combed his thinning grey hair. Self-discipline, patience and routine, were the key to surviving a long sentence in prison and nothing diverted Tom away from his regime. Not even the prospect of seeing the new resident.

After a final look in the mirror, Tom walked back to his cell, put his wash kit on the table and then headed out along the corridor to where Nick Wood was holed up. He knocked on the door but there was no answer. He knocked again and waited.

'Yes?' came a rather timid voice.

'Can I come in?' asked Tom.

'Who is it?'

'Tom Hawks. I'm a friend. I arranged for you to come here.'

Nick sat on his bed listening to the ridiculous claim of the man outside, *'arranged for me to come here.' He must be a raving lunatic,* he thought.

Nick wondered if he should call for help, but he was three floors up. No one would hear him and it might antagonise the man into violence. There seemed little option but to take the risk. He got up, pulled back his bed slightly and pushed the door open a couple of inches. He peered through the crack and saw a middle-aged guy with greying hair standing outside.

'Been looking forward to meeting you Nick,' the man said. Nick wasn't sure what to do, so cautiously he opened the door a few more inches.

'Can I come in?' asked Tom.

'What for?'

'I can tell you why you're here,' he said.

Nick weighed up his options and realising they didn't amount to much, he retreated into the cell but left the door as it was.

'I know prison food's crap but I'm not that skinny, Nick,' said Tom, chuckling as he pulled open the door and pushed the bed back so he could get in.

Nick backed away to a chair against the far wall. When he sat down, he lent forward more than he needed to and with his good hand, quickly undid the laces of one of his boots. He wanted a weapon. In an instant he could now flick off the boot and smash it into the psycho should he come too close. Tom looked on with mild amusement. After a few months in prison, the young lad was bound to have heard a few grisly stories about the lifers.

'Must be a bit nervous being locked away with us lot,' he said trying to break the ice, but from the expression on Nick's face, it hadn't worked.

'Saw you the day you came in,' said Tom. 'You looked as wretched as they come. I can see the main courtyard from my cell. Come on, take a look.' he said

Nick shook his head *No way,* he thought. *I'm staying put.*

Tom couldn't really blame him. Anyway, the explanations were going to be left to someone else and it was time for Tom to go. 'I've got to go to work but I'll see you later,' he said. 'You're with friends now, so try to relax.'

Nick didn't feel like relaxing. He couldn't understand why the man appeared so friendly. But it certainly wasn't the first time he had been fooled by a friendly face since arriving in prison. 'Don't trust no-one,' Dave had told him. Nick didn't intend to. He sat on his bed wondering whether it would be better for him to grass on the Dragon and risk being transferred.

* * *

Half an hour later, Nick was startled by another knock on his cell door. By now everyone should have been at work and he wondered who it could be.

'Who's there?' he asked picking up his boot.

'Amy Jones.'

Nick flung the boot to the floor, grabbed the door handle and yanked it open. In front of him stood Amy.

'How are you?' she asked.

'How do you think? My hand's been busted,' he said holding up his plastered hand. 'And now I'm on the nutter's wing. *You've got to help me,*' he pleaded.

Amy didn't know where to start. She looked behind her at the deserted landing and then looked back at Nick. 'Let me show you something,' she said.

Even though he trusted Amy, he still glanced

nervously up and down the corridor before following her a few steps along the landing to the door of another cell. It wasn't locked and Amy pulled it open. Nick peered in, wondering what possible reason they had for being there, but then he looked at the far wall and his jaw dropped open in surprise. *What the fuck's going on*? he thought to himself in disbelief.

Facing him was the first picture he had painted in Blackthorpe. He recognised it immediately. On the wall next to it there had to be ten others.

'The lifer who came to see you earlier,' said Amy. 'He's your biggest fan.'

* * *

Nick struggled to take it all in. The lifers had a fearful reputation, the men he would least like to meet, yet Amy had explained that the myth surrounding the lifers was just that—a myth. And what's more the lifers were pleased to keep it that way. They were quite happy to be segregated from the rest of the prison and avoid all the aggravation. On their own wing they were able to organise themselves, without the worry of drugs and violence.

'As you can see,' she had said, pulling open the door of the cell next to Nick's. 'None of them even bother to lock their doors.'

Nick was starting to realise that staying on the lifer's wing would not be as bad as he had initially thought. 'But what'll happen when the governor finds out I won't tell him who beat me up?' he asked. 'He'll transfer me.'

'Don't worry about that. We've got a plan to keep you. At least for a while. We've told the governor you've got a chance of winning a prize at the annual education awards. I doubt he'll pass up the opportunity of impressing the Home Office.'

* * *

Tom Hawks went to work that day with lightness

133

in his step he had not had for a long time. He wasn't sure why Nick had ended up in prison, but having seen the boy close up, he knew that he was no big time drug dealer and his reservations had been put to bed. For once, Tom was so excited at the prospect of seeing his protégé at work, he almost forgot he was in prison. It was the shrill blow on a whistle that brought him back to reality.

'Christ, what's going on?' asked Shortie as they made their way across the yard to the entrance of the metal shop. In the distance they saw six guards running to the door of the induction wing.

'No idea,' said Tom watching the scene, and being aware of the Alsatian nearby looking intensely alert.

'Better move on, Shortie,' he said to his friend. 'Les can tell us later. Looks pretty serious though.'

Half an hour later, officer Les Wright wandered into the lifer's department in the metal shop and told Tom what had happened.

'You're not going to like this,' he said shaking his head. 'The grass has nailed Pete Vacanni.'

Tom glanced round at Shortie. Both of them liked Pete. He was a rogue, but a man you could trust. It was to him that Tom had turned to for help when Nick had been interviewed by the governor all those months ago.

'It was his fiftieth birthday,' continued Les. 'Some of the lads had planned a bit of a do tonight, bit of hooch, a joint or two, nothing serious. You know the score Tom. Trouble is someone with a big mouth spread the word and the grass found out.'

'And he sent another note,' guessed Shortie. 'Must have done,' said Les. 'We'd have turned a blind eye, you know that Tom, but the governor insisted. He even came down to help! We found the stuff stashed under Pete's bed. Pete was hauled off down the block to cool off. Some party he'll be having now.'

Tom put down his tea, the smile he'd been wearing now wiped off his face. He had responsibilities. It was all very well hiding away in safety on the lifer's wing enjoying his paintings, but the prison was becoming a dangerous place to live. Not that all the lifers could be trusted. No matter where you were in prison, you had to watch your words, but Tom preferred to be where he was, away from the ever present danger. *Certainly better than on Pete's wing tonight* he thought. He knew that when the prisoners returned from work, one would get the blame for opening their mouth and a fight would start.

Tom had all but given up trying to find the grass, but every now and then, when a new incident occurred, his interest would be rekindled. Once again Tom put his mind to the problem of finding the grass and for the rest of the morning, he thought of little else.

* * *

Nick was sitting alone on his bed inspecting the plaster on his arm, when the door of his cell swung open. As soon as he saw who it was he sat up bolt upright.

'Relax,' said Tom planting himself down on a chair. 'It's been a hard day.'

From outside footsteps approached and Winston's head popped 'round the door. 'Tea's in your cell Tom. I made one for the kid as well.'

Tom levered himself out of his chair. 'I was just getting comfy. Fancy a cuppa Nick?' he asked, as he opened the cell door and headed out without looking back. Feeling more confident Nick got up and followed Tom down the landing to his cell, where once again he was stunned at the sight of his pictures hanging on the wall.

'Your first is my favourite,' said Tom a few

minutes later pointing at the beautifully framed .picture hanging on the far wall. This time Nick walked forward to study it more closely, looking at the range of colours he'd plastered onto the page with a critical eye.

'You could probably do it better now,' said Tom guessing what Nick was thinking. 'But I think it's brilliant. A right breath of fresh air. You've no idea what it's like being banged up for life. It's been twenty years since I last saw any countryside. When Amy showed me the painting it was like taking a walk outside. It was never put up in the visits hall. None of your pictures ever 'ave been. The lads bought 'em all—lock stock and barrel.'

Nick was lost for words, he was flattered but embarrassed at the same time. The pictures were okay but not *that* brilliant. He could definitely do a better job now.

'So tell me, Nick,' said Tom, rolling up some tobacco and lighting up. 'How the hell did a kid like you end up in this shithole?' Nick turned towards Tom. After months in prison and endless sleepless nights, he knew the answer to that question.

'I'm in here because I was fool,' he said.

* * *

That night Nick lay on his bed and tried to imagine what it must be like to spend twenty years in prison. Both of Tom's brothers had died while he'd been locked away. His one sister was in hospital. Worst of all, his mother had passed away several years before and he hadn't been allowed to go to the funeral.

'Last person you want a visit from in prison is the chaplain telling you your mum's passed away,' Tom had said.

It was one of many things that Tom had told him that afternoon. The one thing that stunned him was the ease with which Tom had ended up with a life sentence. He'd thought that anyone serving life would have to be psycho with a string of violence behind them. But Tom was just a thief.

'Just a bit of nickin' at first, down the local shops mostly,' Tom had told him. 'We got away with that, so we went onto bigger things.'

Bigger things in Tom's book meant warehouses and the occasional factory. It was when Tom escalated from simple thieving up to robbing banks, that things took a turn for the worse.

'It was a mate of mine that caused the problem. I can still remember the day he walked into the room with a 'shooter' in his hand saying 'this is the way forward Tom.' Christ I almost shit myself looking down it's double barrel.' It was two years later that someone was shot.

'It was an accident. We never normally loaded 'em,' Tom had told him. Then with what sounded like words born from eternal regret: 'The fuckin' thing just went off.'

Nick had read stories about gangsters and armed robbers, but he never thought he'd ever meet one. Tom didn't seem so bad. He certainly didn't seem to be the sort of guy who would cold bloodedly gun someone down. *Maybe prison had changed him for the better,* he thought.

Nick then wondered if *he'd* changed in any way. He thought back to what he'd been like when he had first entered Blackthorpe. *Thank Christ Jason was a decent bloke. Imagine if I'd had to share with a bloke like Scarface.* Since hiding away from Scarface on the 'smack 'eads' landing, he'd hardly seen anything of the man. In fact he hadn't even thought of him for weeks until that afternoon when officer Les Wright told Tom he'd been transferred. He looked back at how terrified Scarface had made him feel in the early part of his sentence and realised a man gets used to everything in prison—even fear.

Nick let his mind drift. Back it went. Days, weeks, months, then suddenly it jerked to a halt the night he'd been arrested. The night his life had fallen apart. He closed his eyes and tried to conjure up a picture of Jessica, but no longer did her face easily come to mind. Then he thought of what Tom had said. 'You tried to impress your friends and you took a risk. You fucked up good and proper because you didn't have the sense to say 'no'.'

Nick didn't want it to be that simple, but he knew it was. He wanted to blame someone other than himself. But there was no-one else to blame. Tom was right. 'And if you want my advice,' he'd said. 'If you don't toughen up, you'll be a loser all your life. Hard times lie ahead for you when you get released. From now on you've got to make the right choices.' The words rang in Nick's ears until he finally fell into a fitful sleep.

Chapter 13

During the following weeks, the grass in Blackthorpe had a busy time. Sid on the induction wing was done for 'hooch'. Eddie was caught nicking sheets out of the laundry and three guys working in the kitchen were caught smuggling out a month's supply of tinned fruit, but there was no news of who the grass could be. In fact Tom had all but given up trying to find out and spent more and more time watching Nick paint.

Nick's hand had recovered quicker than expected and the doctor had exchanged the heavy plaster for one that enabled him to move his fingers more freely. Amy seemed even more complimentary about his work now than she had been before. She'd told Tom it had changed, taken on a deeper meaning. Impressionist sort of stuff. *Maybe that's because Nick's changed a bit himself,* Tom thought.

No longer were the pictures simply paintings almost as good as photos. Nick had gone one step further, adding his own impression of the scene. 'What the 'ell's that meant to be?' Tom had asked Amy while trying to make out the shapes in one particular painting.

'It shows how his life has disintegrated,' Amy had explained.

When she went on to describe the emotions hidden in the painting, he became even more impressed with the lad. Expressing one's inner feelings wasn't something that the boys on the lifer's wing were used to, but he could see what she meant.

It was a pity Nick's ex-girlfriend Jessica wasn't around to see the latest picture. One afternoon they were sitting in Nick's cell, studying the piece of work. 'You miss her don't you,' Tom said pointing at the semi-human form in the painting, surrounded by clouds and mist

'Try not to. But I do,' he said. He knew he'd never see Jessica again but it was impossible to banish her from his mind completely. Occasionally he'd lie in bed and fantasise about their good times together but that was happening less and less. Nick wondered if memories, like pain and fear diminished in time. He didn't really want to forget about Jessica completely. Tom could see Nick slipping into a trance. 'Got a photo of her?' he asked bringing him back to the present.

'Not a photo exactly,' replied Nick. 'Just a sketch'. He walked to the end of his bed, bent down and from beneath it he took out the bag that contained all his possessions. He fingered through the contents until he found what he was looking for and pulled out a sketch he had made the year before. He studied the likeness and smiled. The nose was too pert, the mouth too wide and the hair was too straight but it wasn't a bad effort. He handed it over to Tom.

'Good looking girl,' he said holding the sketch up to the light. It was the first time he had ever seen one of Nick's attempts at a portrait and he was impressed. His own were pathetic. It was all well and good drawing some obscure landscape, but to capture a human face on paper, and not make it not look like something out of a horror movie, was simply beyond Tom. Anyway, he didn't paint much any more. He preferred watching Nick at work.

'Done many of these?' he asked, nodding at the drawing.

'Not in here,' Nick said turning away, but he then remembered the sketch he'd made of Jason. 'I did one of my first cellmate,' he said.

'Still got it?' asked Tom. Nick nodded, though he hadn't looked at the drawing since Jason had been transferred. He'd stashed it away in his bag for safe keeping and it now lay hidden beneath the mass of letters he'd received from his mum and sister. Nick picked up his bag again and thumbed through the envelopes. It took him a while to find what he was looking for but eventually he pulled out the sketch, unfolded it and put it on the table He looked at the face that stared back. Even though it was a caricature of Jason, the likeness brought back a flood of memories.

'Pity he wasn't around for longer—I liked him,' he said to Tom.

Tom took the drawing and studied the face. Unusually the sketch was in biro, but his mind was distracted from the mechanics of the sketch. *Didn't he know the lad from somewhere?*

'Who is he?' asked Tom.

'Jason Smith—I used to work with him in the laundry.'

'Not the kid who got beaten up?' asked Tom. When Nick nodded, Tom looked at the drawing more closely, wondering where Jason Smith had ended up. *Probably stuck in some dump miles away from home,* he decided. It was a sorry business when the kids got picked on. Tom recalled what had happened and how the governor had tried to con Nick into revealing who had beaten Jason up. Tom remembered how he had persuaded Pete Vacanni to intervene.

Absentmindedly he turned over the drawing and wondered how Jason Smith would be coping without any visits, and probably, without any friends. There was some writing on the back and he idly read the words. At first his mind was on Jason Smith and he missed the significance of what he read. But then he froze.

LIFER BAXTER—HOOCH—WORK—FRIDAY AM

The impact of the words hit home with shattering force. He thought back over the months to when Charlie Baxter had returned from work and had been caught with hooch stuffed in his overalls. 'You read what's on the back of this?' Tom asked, barely managing to keep the excitement out of his voice.

Nick shook his head. 'Never bothered to look,' he said. 'Jason told me it was rubbish.'

'*Rubbish!*' exclaimed Tom, holding out the note. Nick took a pace forward and read the words. After a few moments his mouth fell open in surprise.

'You'd better tell me exactly what happened the day this was found,' said Tom.

Nick sat down on his bed and thought back to the day in the laundry. 'Jason found it in the jeans he had to wash,' he explained.

'Why didn't Jason tell you what was in the

note. He must have realised what it was?' Nick sat in silence until the answer came to him. *Jason had seen the words all right, but to him they were rubbish.* 'He couldn't read,' said Nick quietly.

'He *what*?' said Tom.

'He couldn't read or write. But I didn't know at the time,' added Nick quickly. 'He told me it was rubbish—I believed him.'

'How did you find out he couldn't read?' asked Tom.

'The doctor told me when I suggested to Jason that we write to each other. I just never put two and two together.' Tom looked at Nick, who was silent for a few seconds. He could almost see Nick putting everything together; connecting up the dots. A look of sheer surprise finally came across his face.

'You know who the grass is,' said Tom.

Nick nodded, stunned by the impact of his discovery.

'Who did the jeans belong to Nick? *Who beat up Jason?* insisted Tom.

Nick was hardly able to believe what he was about to say. He looked Tom straight in the eye. 'The Dragon' he said.

* * *

That night, an hour before 'bang up', Tom and his trusted allies sat in his cell for a reconvening of the war council. The note written by the Dragon lay on his table in front of them. Shortie had read it first and sat with a look of disbelief on his face.

'Jesus, he's the last person I'd 'ave suspected,' he said. 'But why?'

'Not hard to work out,' said Tom addressing the group. 'He does a deal with the governor to grass up the cons, in return he gets a few back-handers. I guess that's how it started. The governor probably doesn't even realise he's dealing in 'smack' and runs a protection racket. Just thinks he's given him a nice cushy job.'

'So what do we do now?' asked Winston, after they had all had a chance to digest the news.

'For the moment we tell no one. Not even the other lifers. You know how word slips out,' said Tom. 'We believe Nick's story, but the rest of the guys might not, specially the smack 'eads on the other wings. The Dragon's the last person they'll want to get rid of. He's their only supply. We've gotta *prove* that he's the grass.'

'How do we do that?' asked Shortie.

'We set a trap for him,' said Tom. 'We'll give him some information that only he could know. If he passes it on, it'll prove to everyone what he is. But it means taking a bit of a risk,' he continued getting to his feet. 'We've gotta sell him a story and there's only one person who can do that.'

'Where are you going?' asked Shortie.

'To have a word with the person who going to feed the Dragon,' said Tom opening the door and walking towards Nick's cell. He had a plan. He just hoped it would work.

* * *

Rain was lashing down outside when Nick found himself on the hospital ward for the second time in just under a month. He was waiting for the governor to visit him. Tom had told him the plan, but it seemed suicidal, and as he waited to be interviewed, he was becoming increasingly nervous about his short-term safety. Finally the door swung open and the governor appeared. He walked over to where Nick was sitting, drew up a chair and sat down.

'So 582. The doctor tells me you've finally recovered your memory,' he said. It was important for the governor to clear up as many assaults as he could before the inspectors visit and he was eager to find out who was responsible. 'So who broke your fingers?' he said getting straight to the point.

Nick paused for a moment. It was the point of no return. 'The man they called Scarface,' he said sealing his fate.

The governor hesitated while he analysed this revelation. It was common knowledge that Styles, better known as Scarface, had been transferred only a few days before. It seemed more than a co-incidence that Wood should recover his memory now. But if it was Styles, it was too late to convict him, as he was no longer in the prison. Yet the case would be solved. It was very good news for the governor.

'So you could remember, but were too scared to tell me before?' asked the governor.

Nick nodded.

'Excellent,' he said. It was the perfect result for the governor and he fought hard to keep the smile of satisfaction off his face. 'You know I'll have to put you back on your old wing now,' he said. Returning to his old wing was an essential part of Tom's plan and the thought appalled Nick but it was now too late to backtrack.

'Yes Sir,' he said.

The governor got up, turned his back on Nick and walked out of the medical centre. He didn't fully trust Nick Wood. After all, he'd been living with the lifers for a few weeks. *God knows what habits he picked up from them,* he thought. But the fact that Wood 582 named Scarface as his attacker was good news. Now he could tie up that investigation and still keep the boy in the prison to try to win him an award. For once he was looking forward to the prison inspectors' visit. No way he'd need to be subservient to those stuck up pratts from the Home Office. Normally he detested the day—but this time he could be very proud of what he was achieving at Blackthorpe.

Chapter 14

Nick entered his old cell on the induction wing and guessed that Dave Walker, his former cellmate, was at work. Nick had told Tom the only way he'd go back to his old wing was if Tom could swing it so he shared with Dave again. It was bad enough having to go back to the wing at all, let alone if he had to share with some nutter. It had taken all Tom's reserves of tobacco to fix it, but somehow Nick was back in the cell he had originally shared with Jason. On one hand it was comforting to return to familiar surroundings, he had nothing to fear from Dave, and Tom seemed to know what he was doing. The lifer had confidence in his plan. But still, so many things could go wrong. There were so many ways the plan could backfire. Try as he might, he couldn't ignore the uneasy feeling of pending disaster.

He perched himself on the bottom bunk and massaged his injured hand. Before he'd left the hospital ward, the doctor had cut off the remaining plaster and for the first time in weeks Nick was able to stretch out his fingers. Even though he had found a way to hold a brush, it had been almost impossible to carry out detailed work. Now his hand was free he just hoped the skills he'd developed before the 'accident' were still there. He didn't want to let Amy down.

'Prison is a terrible place,' she'd said to him recently when talking about the importance of the education award. 'Most inmates have no hope at all. Many of them can't even read or write. If you can show them it's possible to achieve something, even in prison, it might give them hope for the future.' When she'd talked about inmates not being able to read, he had immediately thought of Jason, and it had seemed apt that it was his friend who should be the main subject of his painting. Nick was determined to try his hardest to win an award, not just for himself, but for Amy and all the prisoners in Blackthorpe. He couldn't wait to try out his hand and start the painting after weeks of being bandaged up, but first he had to survive the next few hours and the most dangerous part of Tom's plan.

Nick lent down and picked up his bag of possessions that had already been delivered by the guards and stashed it under his bed. He didn't bother to unpack. If events took a turn for the worse, it would mean a quick evacuation was necessary. He lay back on the bed and waited. Every time he heard footsteps outside, his heart beat faster, but as the minutes ticked by and lunch time came when the door finally opened, he wasn't worried as he knew who it was.

'Heard you were coming back,' said Dave, looking at him suspiciously as he entered the cell for the break. 'There's a few rumours going around that you fell out with the lifers. That true?' he asked pulling off the sweater he was wearing and putting it down on the table.

Nick unbuttoned the sleeve of his shirt and cut the stitching with his plastic knife. Carefully he prized out the letter that had been concealed there since leaving the lifer's wing. Tom hadn't let him carry it in case he was searched by a guard, or worse, the Dragon found it. He handed over the note to Dave, who read the words then smiled, 'I didn't want to believe what they were saying,' he said.

Nick shrugged. He hadn't liked this part of Tom's plan, but the lifer had told him it was essential that all the inmates on Nick's wing believed he'd fallen out with the lifers, or his story wouldn't be believed by the person they had to convince. At work that morning Charlie and Shortie had been busy spreading rumours.

* * *

An hour after lunch, Nick was sitting on the chair in the cell when he heard footsteps outside and he braced himself. He knew who the footsteps belonged to. Although he was scared about what could happen, he was glad the plan was now in motion and there was no turning back. Waiting had been worse than he had expected. The door swung open and the Dragon entered. His bulk filled the cell. He took a pace forward and put his face close to Nick's. 'So you've returned,' he said menacingly, looking Nick up and down.

It was the first time Nick had seen the Dragon since his fingers had been torn from their sockets and involuntarily he re-lived the excruciating flash of pain.

'What I wanna know is why I haven't got the Governor breathing down my neck,' the Dragon said, moving so close to Nick their faces were inches apart. 'He wouldn't have let you back on this wing without you tellin' him who bust yer fingers.'

'I told him Scarface did it,' said Nick. He was trying to remain calm but he could feel the palms of his hands sweating up and his voice sounded high, as though someone else was speaking 'I don't want to be transferred. My visits are too important. It's the only way I could stay in the prison.'

'Why didn't you stay where you were? Word 'ad it you were sorted with a nice little number on the lifer's wing.'

'Things change,' said Nick looking at the floor.

'Rumours true are they?' asked the Dragon. 'They say you're a grass.'

'A couple of the lifers caught me listening outside a cell, that's all. But I'm no grass,' said Nick.

'Then what were you listening for?' he asked

'They'd started picking on me. I wanted to know what they were going to do next.'

The Dragon gave him a knowing smirk. 'You know what they're really like then,' he said.

'They're all bastards,' said Nick. 'They don't care about anything except themselves and their stupid parties.'

The Dragon took his eyes away from Nick and walked to the far side of the cell. From out of his pocket he took a large joint, put it to his lips and lit up. He inhaled deeply and casually blew out a series of smoke rings. 'What sort of parties?' he said.

'They're always having them. They've got one coming up soon. You know the lifer they call Shortie?' Nick asked.

The Dragon nodded.

'It's his birthday bash. Dope, hooch, extra food—the lot. Going to be a right special do, but they never let me join in. They just make me clean up afterwards.'

'I tell yer, they're all like that,' said the Dragon. He took a deep drag from his joint. 'When is the little runt's birthday bash?' he asked casually.

'Same day the prison inspectors are coming,' replied Nick.

'How do you know when that is?'

'Because the governor wants me to do a painting that'll win Blackthorpe an education award. He wants to show the inspectors my picture when they come here. The education department says that's on June 18th—two weeks time. Don't know how the lifers found out but they said it would be a good time to throw a party, cause all the screws would be too busy to search any cells.'

The Dragon had heard enough. He took one last drag of the joint, blew a smoke ring out for good measure and then ground out the joint on the wall. He turned round to Nick. 'I don't give a toss about the lifers, or the inspection,' he said. 'You just start painting again so you can pay your debts.' With that he swept out of the cell and left Nick alone.

Nick got up out of his chair and took a deep breath. He ran his hands through his hair that had become damp with sweat and then wiped them on his trousers. If the Dragon hadn't believed his story, it could have been curtains for him there and then, but it seemed the Dragon had taken the bait - hook, line and sinker. The information about the lifer's party had now been passed on and only time would tell if the Dragon used it and condemned himself. Nick didn't feel a hint of sympathy at the thought of what might happen to him if he did. He'd suffered too much at the hands of the Dragon, and he hoped it was the beginning of the end for his tormentor.

* * *

The next day, several new pots of paint and sheets of paper were delivered to Nick's cell. Amy had told the governor that she thought it best Nick work there on his painting for the education award and the governor had agreed. Nick was quite happy about it too. He wanted the minimum of distractions if he was to do a good job.

'Go on then, what are you painting?' asked Dave as he was getting ready to go to work in the afternoon. 'Word's goin' round you're in for some competition.'

'Just a normal prison scene in here,' Nick said.

Dave had seen quite a few of Nick's paintings and liked the outside scenes best.

'Waste of time painting something in this shithole' he said.

Nick hadn't told Dave that his picture was also part of Tom's plan. He shrugged. 'Wait till it's finished,' he said.

Dave grunted and walked out the door leaving Nick on his own to concentrate.

* * *

At the same time that Nick started painting, the governor was sitting in his office finishing off some paperwork, when there was a knock on the door. He hated being disturbed when he had things to do. 'Yes,' he said impatiently.

An officer entered and walked over to the desk. 'I've got some letters from the inmates for you, Sir,' he said putting the envelopes down. The governor looked at them and flicked a nod of thanks in the direction of the man, then waved his hand in dismissal.

When the officer had left, the governor reached forward and picked up the letters. No doubt the usual array of complaints. Some were almost justified, he thought, but normally the letters were anonymous and too rude to repeat to anyone. Without much care he ripped open the first few, briefly read the contents and discarded most in the bin. *What do they want?* he asked himself. *They commit a crime and then expect some paradise inside.* Bored with his task he flicked through to the end of the pile, ready to discard them in the bin but his eyes narrowed as he recognised the handwriting on one of the last envelopes. This was the only type of letter he enjoyed receiving from inmates. He tore open the envelope and took out the note inside.

'LIFERS WING—DAY OF INSPECTORS VISIT—TOP FLOOR—DRUGS PARTY

By now the governor was used to the brevity of the grass's notes; straight to the point and rarely wrong. He read the note again and let the information sink in.

This would indeed be a feather in his cap. Not only would the inspectors see a well run prison, but they would be able to experience, first hand, one of the governor's coups. Added to that, if Wood 582 could produce a top class painting, as a demonstration of a thriving education department, it would indeed be a special day.

The governor locked the note away in the prison safe and made an entry in his diary. For some time he'd been after one of the plum jobs in the prison service. One of the large London prisons would be the perfect place for him to end up. Perhaps this would go some way to securing that. A smile spread across his thin lips. He sat back in his chair, relaxed and thought of the house he would buy, somewhere near Clapham on the south side of the river Thames. Somewhere handy for HMP Potsdown.

Chapter 15

Tom Hawks woke up early on the day of the prison inspectors' visit and lay in bed nervously thinking about his plan to expose the Dragon. Several hours later, he still felt nervous as he stood by his cell window, looking down at the governor and the prison inspectors. He'd finished work not less than an hour before and now he and the other lifers were locked away on the wing.

He watched as the governor showed the inspectors round the outside of the prison and then into the laundry that had been specially cleaned and tidied. Tom knew the governor would only let the inspectors see areas of the prison that had been carefully prepared for their visit. *They'd never see the smack 'eads wing in a month of Sundays*, thought Tom to himself, *unless we forced the issue*. The parts of the prison they *needed* to see would be closed off for the day on some carefully thought up health and safety rule, and with most of the prisoners locked away out of sight, there was no one around to tell them what Blackthorpe was really like.

As Tom watched the scene below, he wondered

for the umpteenth time whether his plan would work. When he had originally found out the truth about the Dragon, he had considered simply confronting the monster with the note he'd written about Charlie Baxter, but Shortie had talked him out of that.

'What happens if we show it to 'im and he just tears it up or one of the other smack 'eads does? Then it would be Nick's word against his.'

So Tom had come up with a more complex plan, that would not only expose the Dragon, but hopefully all the rotten decay in Blackthorpe. It was a prison run by drug gangs with danger lurking at every corner. It was a demoralising hellhole where rehabilitation was nonexistent and someone should be told what was going on.

In preparation, he and Nick Wood had painted two pictures that would be at the heart of the plan. The painting Nick had produced would be seen by the prison inspectors later in the day and was entered for the prison education awards. Tom's large painting would be seen by all the inmates on the Dragon's wing.

Only that morning he had carefully folded up his extra large picture and smuggled it underneath his overalls into the metal shop, where he had secretly given it to Dave Walker. It was his job to hang it up in the canteen later that afternoon. If all went well it would be the nail in the coffin for the Dragon. *If all goes badly,* thought Tom *it could be curtains for us and a quick transfer to boot.*

Tom took a deep breath and forced himself to smile. It was finally time to set the plan in motion. On cue, the door opened, Winston entered and saw the pile of goodies lying on Tom's bed. 'Nice one. It's been a while since Shortie's seen a spread like this,' he said.

Tom picked up an armful of crisps, biscuits, bread and some special treats that would surely bring a smile to Shortie's face. 'Give us a hand', said Tom.

Winston bent down and gathered up the bottles of drink that had been specially prepared. Together they struggled down the corridor towards the end cell, kicking on several doors as they went. By the time they reached Shortie's cell, four other inmates had joined them.

'Time to party,' said Tom loudly as he pushed open the door and looked at his friend. 'Happy birthday,' he said, winking. Winston followed him into the cell, dropped his arm full of goodies onto the bed and let everyone pass him into the small room.

'Jesus! The last supper?' said Shortie looking at the pile of food.

'Let's hope it's not,' said Tom. 'Come on everyone, tuck in. Make the most of it.' Shortie grabbed a packet of crisps and a bottle of drink. The others dived into the pile and before long the party was in full swing.

Outside on the landing, a guard specially chosen for duty on the lifer's wing that day was listening to the noise. He had been told to report directly to the governor when the party started. When another peel of laughter broke out he decided it was time. Quietly he made his way to the ground floor and took out his radio.

* * *

At the same time as the lifer's party was starting, Nick Wood was sitting at the end of his bed looking at the picture he had finished two days before. Dave had just left for the canteen where he had a job to do for Tom, and Nick was left alone thinking about the next few hours.

Finally the big day had arrived. The day his specially painted picture would be seen by the inspectors and hopefully justice, if there was any, would be served.

He thought back to the advice Amy Jones

had given him. 'Every picture should tell a story.' He looked at his painting a final time and couldn't help wondering about his friend Jason Smith; where he was and how he was getting on.

The subject of the painting had been Tom's idea, and initially Nick and Amy had been shocked by the suggestion. But after listening to Tom, and realising the chance they were being given to help make a change, they had gone along with the idea.

'It might make the inspectors want to see the full picture instead of just what they're shown,' Tom had argued. He had also pointed out, rather worryingly for Nick, that if all went wrong, Nick and he might be transferred out of Blackthorpe in the first available 'sweat box'.

The painting was due to be seen by the inspectors later that afternoon when they visited the art department and he hoped they were inquisitive men. Carefully he covered his work with a sheet and then holding it under his arm, he headed out the cell door to the education department.

* * *

On the other side of the prison, the governor was in his office drinking tea with the inspectors. They had already been shown the outside of the prison and were now talking about the discipline within the walls themselves.

'We're very pleased to see that a couple of recent assaults were solved. Let's hope you keep up the good work,' said Peters, one of the three inspectors. 'All we're a little concerned about, is the apparent lack of educational encouragement in the prison.'

The governor was so confident that everything was going his way he decided not to grovel any more. 'Significant improvements have recently been made as you'll soon see. Let's not forget, gentleman that this is a prison and first and foremost it should be a place of punishment. I'm all for creating opportunities but surely they have to be earned,' he said. 'Now perhaps...' The governor was interrupted by a loud knock on the door. 'Come in,' he called. An officer walked in with a stern expression on his face.

'The party on the lifer's wing has started, sir,' he said.

The governor turned to the inspectors. 'Gentleman, keeping a tight rein on the inmates is a difficult job, as you know. But we try hard in Blackthorpe, particularly with our lifers. If you remember from my report, we've allowed some of the teachers to give them separate lessons on the education block. Now you'll see how we're repaid.' The governor's face took on a solemn expression. 'It's come to our attention that substance abuse is taking place on the lifer's wing this very minute. A very serious offence as I know you're aware.'

The governor rose out of his chair. He now felt completely in control. 'I must oversee this operation. Perhaps you would like to accompany me,' he said, dramatically sweeping out of the room. The head of the inspection team nodded at his two colleagues and they got up and followed.

Ten minutes later the governor, ten officers and two powerful attack dogs gathered quietly at the bottom of the stairs on the lifer's wing. Surprise meant everything.

'Now men,' said the governor in hushed tones standing on the first step so all could see. The inspectors looked on intently. 'When the whistle goes, dogs in first—then you men go in with batons drawn. He looked at the faces of all the officers to see if they understood, then turned and climbed purposefully up the three flights of stairs. The officers who followed weren't quite as confident. The theory of cell searches is all well and good, but the practise often leaves a lot to be desired. Too many had gone wrong in the past, for the men not to be slightly nervous.

When they reached the top landing, the governor spoke quietly to the officer who had resumed his post and was keeping guard. 'There's about seven lifers in there sir,' he whispered. 'Sounds as if they're really tanked up.'

The governor nodded and signalled for his men to divide into two groups, one each side of the door with the dogs up front. He took a last look at his men, took a deep breath and gave a short sharp blast on his whistle.

* * *

Nick Wood and Amy Jones were watching the raid take place from a window in the art department. They'd seen the officers gather outside and had watched them follow the governor in with the dogs. The first sign that something had gone disastrously wrong was when they saw the doctor hurrying across the yard below. *No one should have got hurt in the raid*, thought Nick. Not long after that they heard a siren, quickly followed by the sight of an ambulance coming to a stop outside the lifer's wing. They watched as two paramedics, carrying a stretcher, climbed down from the ambulance and rushed into the building.

For several long minutes nothing happened, then the paramedics came out carrying the stretcher, on top of which lay a man covered with a blanket. All that was visible was a head poking out the top.

'Can you see who it is?' asked Nick. Amy strained her eyes but shook her head. They were too far away.

With the stretcher safely on board, the ambulance pulled out of the main gates and screamed off into the distance. Nick and Amy continued to watch the scene below but no one else came out of the building and Nick had seen enough. He turned away. Whatever had happened the plan had gone wrong. Someone had been hurt and no matter how Nick looked at it, that was bad news.

'What do we do now?' he said to Amy.

'You'd better go back,' she said looking alarmed. 'When something like this happens it's best to be on the wing.' Nick was on the point of asking what she thought had happened but realised she knew no more than he did. He took a final look out of the window. *Nothing could go wrong* he'd told himself. But it was obvious that something had.

* * *

From the other side of the main courtyard, the Dragon watched the ambulance roar away with a smile of satisfaction written across his face. Nothing in the whole of his prison experience had given him such enjoyment. Nailing the lifers was bound to get him a few favours from the governor, but equally he was looking forward to seeing the devastated expressions on the faces of those that were caught. *Hopefully the pious gits would all get knocked back a few years,* he thought to himself. With an injury bad enough for an ambulance to turn up, no matter what had happened, the lifers were in big trouble.

For special occasions the Dragon had a small bottle of whisky stashed away inside his mattress. He crossed the cell, closed the door making sure the Weasel couldn't see in and ripped open the stitching. He took out the bottle of whisky, undid the top and let his nose savour the smell. Then, from off the table he picked up his mug and poured himself a generous shot. It was a long time since he'd really had a cause for celebration. As he put the cup to his lips and took a sip of the golden liquid, he couldn't keep the grin off his face. *I just hope the injuries are fuckin' bad,* he thought as he returned to the window for his ringside seat.

* * *

At the same time as the Dragon was sipping his whisky, the doctor was returning to the medical centre from the emergency scene. When he reached his office he opened up the door with his keys, locked it behind him and made a beeline for his medicine cabinet. He reached in and took out a small bottle, picked up a tumbler from the sink and poured himself a large brandy. He always allowed himself a 'nerve steadier' after an emergency, but this time it was more of a celebration drink.

At first, when he had received the call saying a man had been injured during the raid, he had been fearful of what he would find. But when he had reached the top landing on the lifer's wing and saw the lack of commotion, he knew nothing serious could have happened. A crowd of guards stood idly chatting; no inmates were pinned to the ground by officers or dogs, no pools of blood lay on the floor. Yet he could definitely hear someone groaning.

'Doctor coming through,' he'd said loudly, making sure everyone stood back. It was then he'd seen the governor lying on the floor. Immediately he'd turned to the nearest officer, 'What happened?' he had asked, alarmed by the sight. Thoughts of what would happen to any inmate who'd hurt the governor flashed though his mind; a year or two added onto a sentence; a transfer back to maximum security. It was a deadly serious situation.

'Governor took a fall Doc,' the officer had said.

'*A fall?*' exclaimed the doctor.

'Yeah, that's all doc. The dogs went in first, bit excited like and knocked over a bottle of drink. Orange squash I think it was. The governor then came charging in like a madman and slipped. Must've got his foot jammed under the table somehow. I think he's bust his leg, there was this almighty *crack* when he went down.'

The doctor had made his way into the cell, put down his medical bag on the bed and bent down to inspect the governor. He was aware that three other men were in the cell with him, inspectors he guessed by their smart suits, but his mind focused on his patient who was groaning loudly.

'Lie still—I'm going to cut off the trouser leg,' he'd said taking out a pair of scissors from his bag.

'*No, no, don't touch me,*' the governor had cried out.

'Come on now,' said the doctor knowing that the worst broken leg was not more painful or horrific as many of the injuries he saw in the prison. He was always staggered at the bravery of the youngsters who hobbled and crawled their way to his surgery for treatment after being given a severe beating. A wave of anger had swept through him. Taking no notice of the whimpering, and no longer showing the compassion he might have, he started cutting the trouser leg away with a pair of scissors.

Once the leg was exposed it hadn't taken much of his medical knowledge to see it was broken. It was bent at an odd angle and he could see it was a bad fracture. The guard had been right. Somehow the foot must have been trapped as the governor slipped and the leg had been snapped by the force of his own weight. 'It's a nasty break—definitely a hospital case. You might well have to stay in for some time,' he added, trying to sound concerned.

The doctor had stayed long enough to oversee the work carried out by the paramedics, who had arrived with the ambulance, and was on the point of leaving, when one of the inspectors asked if they could have a word. 'Somewhere quiet and private?' the inspector had suggested.

'Use my cell if you like,' said Tom who was

standing next to officer Les Wright.

The doctor had nodded his thanks and led the inspectors along the corridor. Inside Tom's cell the inspectors had quizzed him for well over half an hour, and he had been encouraged to speak freely. He told them how many kids he had to stitch up each week, battered to pulp by the gangs. He told them about the drug problems in Blackthorpe and finally he said that in his opinion, nearly every patient treated was due to violence on the wings and not accidents as were normally reported.

The inspectors were shocked by what they heard and also by how far Blackthorpe had apparently fallen into decay since the previous visit. 'Is there anything else we need to know?' they had asked. 'You should go to see Amy Jones in the art department,' the doctor had told them. Back in his office he took another sip of his drink and without a hint of guilt, grinned like a Cheshire cat.

* * *

At five o'clock that night, the cell doors were unlocked and the inmates were allowed down for tea. Nick and Dave Walker joined the back of the queue that slowly descended to the ground floor. Everyone was talking about the raid, there was no other topic of conversation.

Nick collected his meal and made his way to a table on the far side of the canteen. Dave was close behind. They sat together hardly saying a word and just listened to the spreading rumours. One inmate thought an inspector had been killed, another was sure a guard had been stabbed. Someone else had heard that a lifer was dead. Only Nick and Dave knew the truth. Amy had visited them just before she'd finished for the day and had explained in detail what had happened.

'After talking to the doctor the inspectors came

to see me,' she said to Nick.

'In the education department?' he asked.

Amy nodded. 'I showed them your painting, it stunned them. They asked so many questions they stayed for ages. Then they demanded to see the scene of the painting.'

Nick thought back to his picture. The painting was of the smack 'eads landing. A place that Tom Hawks had said it was their duty to try to expose. It showed Jason lying on the floor after he had passed out on heroin surrounded by squalor and decay. A usual prison scene, Nick had told Dave, and that was exactly what he had painted. *If the inspectors saw that landing*, Nick thought to himself, *then they really would have something to be shocked about*

Dave nudged Nick in the arm. 'Time to expose the Dragon. Let 'em see Tom's painting,' he said. He got up and walked over to the far wall near the exit. There he took hold of a length of cord he had left earlier, pulled it, and stood back as the large picture unfurled. Then, casually, he walked back to sit down beside Nick where they both waited.

It didn't take long before an inmate stood underneath the painting taking a closer look. Nick looked towards the Dragon's table to see if anyone was paying attention, but as usual the Dragon was smiling as he surveyed the canteen, *probably looking for his next victim,* he thought.

Nick glanced back at Tom's picture. Being at the far side of the room, he was too far away to see the detail of the painting, but when he glanced at some of the inmates sitting nearer, he could see them pointing up at it and talking earnestly amongst themselves. It was then that Dave Walker stood up and wandered over. He was joined by one or two others who also wanted a closer look. After a few seconds Nick joined the group himself.

At first the Dragon was unconcerned. For the past week he had been used to the inmates looking at the stupid pictures. It had been part of the governor's plan to show a thriving happy prison to the inspectors. But he started to become agitated when the group of inmates in front of him kept growing. Some were pointing at him, others were whispering to each other, but none were smiling. The Dragon's eyes narrowed. That was unusual. The pictures had been so dreadful, at least it had given everyone a laugh. But not anymore it seemed. Overcome by curiosity, the Dragon finally got to his feet and walked out to the front of the group where he could see the picture for himself.

Nick watched the Dragon's jaw drop open in stunned disbelief. Amy had obviously given Tom the same lesson he had received—that every picture should tell a story. Jason Smith, his friend, could be clearly seen lying on the floor in the laundry, blood on the floor with the Dragon standing above him. The note grassing up Charlie Baxter was there to be read and something that was impossible for anyone to know about, except the Dragon, the lifer's party. It was impossible not to understand what the picture was saying and it was signed, not just by Tom Hawks, but by many of the lifers and importantly, Dave Walker, one of the most trusted inmates in the prison. It was proof beyond doubt that the grass had been identified, and it proved beyond doubt that the grass was the Dragon.

For long moments no-one moved and an eerie silence descended over the group as everyone was coming to the same conclusion. Then Pete Vacanni looked across at Nick. 'You only told one person about the party?'

Nick hesitated. He knew that he was about to condemn a man to a brutal beating, and he stood debating what to do but then he looked up at Tom's painting and saw Jason lying in his own blood. It was enough to condemn the Dragon. 'Yeah. Only one person.' he said.

Knowing something drastic was happening, the Weasel walked forward to stand next to his leader, but when he saw the picture his face drained of blood. Slowly he inched himself away to the back of the group, but no one took any notice of him as every eye was now turned in one direction. They were all looking at the Dragon.

'You bastard! So you're the fuckin' grass,' said Pete Vacanni, spitting out the words with venom. Suddenly the silence had been broken—and with it the spell.

The Dragon sprinted towards the door where guards could normally be found, but to his horror he found there was no one there. For a split second he froze with panic, but it was long enough for an arm to lock round his chest and another round his legs. In wild desperation his hands flew out like grappling hooks and locked onto the door frame, but within seconds they were prized open. A hand from behind then clamped itself over his mouth and slowly, but surely, he was dragged back into the canteen.

Dave Walker put his hand on Nick's shoulder. 'Best get out of here. No good you seeing this.' he said, guiding Nick towards the door and the stairs. 'Go and do some painting. Leave this to us lot.' After watching Nick start to climb up, he turned round, closed door of the canteen behind him, and went back to help serve up prison justice.

Chapter 16

A month after the Dragon had been released from hospital and transferred to a prison where solitary confinement awaited, Nick found out he had won an award for his painting. Two weeks after that, he sat on the stage in the prison gym, waiting for the presentation ceremony to begin. It was attended by the local press, prison officers, fellow inmates and staff from the education department. Even Nick's mother and sister had been allowed in for the afternoon. Blackthorpe had a new governor and he was proving to be very good. Since the Grim Reaper had been removed, due to a damning report by the inspectors, Amy and the education department had received more funding. A drug rehabilitation unit was to be built, and active anti-bullying campaign was already in operation throughout the prison. Now inmates could concentrate on the future rather than their survival.

Sitting on a chair several rows back from the stage, Tom looked up at Nick. He was going to miss the lad when he was released and that wouldn't be too long by his calculations. Still, if the new governor proved to be as good as he looked, Tom might even get a move himself soon. He smiled. *Be patient you old fool,* he told himself. But at the same time he found it hard not to long for the outside world. He had taken such an interest in art, all he wished for was freedom and a chance to save up some money so he could visit a famous art gallery. He was due for parole in four years and that was nothing to a lifer.

On stage Nick was reflecting on his time inside. With only weeks to go before he was due for release it looked like he was going to make it safely through his sentence and it was mainly down to Tom, and a bit of luck. No longer was there a protection racket running in the prison. The canteen queue had been sorted out and the smack 'eads landing had been cleaned up. Inmates could now go round the prison without fearing for their lives. It was no holiday camp, but it was safer. Tom's plan had worked out better than anyone could have expected.

Three days before his lifer friend had given him what he'd said was his last lecture, but the way Tom had carried on during the last month he thought that unlikely. This time Tom had shown him a newspaper article. 'Sixth Form College Student Gets Three Years for 'E's,' read the headline. Nick had read the article with interest. It was a similar case to his own. But unlike himself, the young man still had his sentence stretching ahead of him.

Reading the article had given Nick an opportunity to reflect how lucky he'd been. There were one hundred and thirty prisons in the country but there were very few inmates who bothered to help others as Tom had done, but there was always someone like the Dragon. Normally the kids would have to fend for themselves and Nick realised how fortunate he'd been. Without Tom's help he could well have drifted down a slippery slope. *No way I'm ever coming back here again,* he thought.

A loud tap on a table made him look round and he saw the governor getting up to make his speech. The governor was a tall man with broad shoulders and a clear loud voice. 'We're here today to acknowledge the talent of a young man who has managed to spend his time constructively in prison against considerable odds. We all know...'

Nick started off listening but his attention was drawn to the picture resting on the stand to one side. An officer had just taken off the cloth that had been covering it up. His painting been sent away to London for assessment by the judges and it was the first time he'd seen it in well over a month.

Like Tom's picture it told a story and as he looked at it memories came flooding back. He'd been so scared when he had first set foot in Blackthorpe, but sharing cells with Jason had really helped. Until two weeks before he'd not heard anything about his friend and thought he never would. That was until the new governor stepped in. On hearing how the young man had suffered at the hands of the Dragon, he'd found out which prison Jason had been sent to, and on the promise he would attend a drug course, he arranged for his transfer back to Blackthope. It was a move that had a big effect on many of the inmates. No longer did they feel they were just a name and a number.

Jason had arrived back in the prison only a few days before. Nick had gone to visit him in the medical centre when Jason was being checked over. His ribs were still painful and the scar on his chin looked fresh. Nick had been worried his friend had changed.

'How are you?' he'd asked.

'I 'ad to pretend I was a Liverpool supporter and speak in a scouser accent for the last few months. And they eat black pudding for breakfast! How d'you think I feel.

Jason had survived in a tough Liverpool prison and proved he was the ultimate survivor.

Nick looked up towards the back of the hall and spotted his friend. He smiled at Jason and the young man winked back. Both had tough journeys ahead of them and Nick hoped his friend would arrive safely. Unlike himself, Jason had an excuse for being in prison. He'd had a lousy upbringing and was at the other end of the scale where privilege was concerned. That's what Tom had made him realise. Nick had everything as a youngster and blew it. Now he was being given a second chance. He knew his mum and sister would support him when he was released, and with a reference from Amy he had already secured himself a place at a new art college. With the help he was being given he had it made compared to someone like Jason, and the rest of society had it made compared to someone like Nick.

'You've got a criminal record now. If you don't make money painting it'll be tough getting a job doing anything else,' Tom had pointed out. 'You've been in prison. No one wants to employ an ex-con.' It was this warning that had made Nick start to worry about his future. It was great hearing nice comments from the governor about him and his painting but they would count for nothing when he was released. The art students he'd be competing against had a head start. If he couldn't make up the time he'd be in trouble.

In the back of his mind he heard the governor call out his name. He got up and made his way forward listening to the applause, dazed by the flash of lights as photographs were taken. He knew everyone was congratulating him for his picture, but he knew they were also wishing him luck for the future. He shook hands with the governor and then stood back to one side. He tried to focus on what the governor was saying but he couldn't. His mind was distracted by the journey that faced him. It was going to be tough when he was released and he didn't want to let anyone down. He turned his head and looked at the sea of people below to find a source of strength and inspiration. Naturally his eyes gravitated to the row of lifers and Tom. Throughout his sentence Tom had been there to help him out no matter what the problem. He looked down at his friend, but instead of seeing the show of friendly support he'd expected, the lifer stared back with a look of granite on his face.

Tom could see Nick looking at him from the stage and he wanted to smile back but he deliberately kept his expression impassive. He was so proud of the lad. He was also pretty pleased with himself for keeping the kid safe, but from now on Nick would be on his own. In little more than a month all the temptations would be there again. He'd meet another Jessica who he'd fall head over heels for. He'd go to some party, have a few drinks and then all the lessons he should have learned would be put to the test.

His brother once had a dog that was too timid. Kept on running back when he should have been out hunting. His brother had turned his back on him and the dog had turned out tough and brave. *Sometimes it's kind to be cruel,* he thought to himself. For his last days in prison there'd be no more back up for the kid. If Nick hadn't learned his lesson by now he was in deep trouble because it was time to fly the nest. Besides, there was now someone else in the prison he'd be watching over.

The cool look on the lifer's face had a sobering effect on Nick. Physically he'd become stronger in prison but it was now time to toughen up mentally. He was responsible for throwing away what he had, now it was up to him to put things right. There was going to be no safety net for him in the outside world. His destiny lay in his own hands. He looked at the picture next to him that he had he had painted of his friend and remembered how Jason had told him to be positive. 'Tell 'em you're a budding Picasso,' he'd said. A look of determination appeared on Nick's face. The answer was simple. Tough as it was going to be he couldn't afford self doubt. *It's down to me now,* he thought.

When Nick looked back at the lifer it was as though he saw Tom for the first time. He shut his eyes to capture the bone structure of the jaw, the deep lines on the face born through years of regret, and the suspicious eyes of a man who'd spent twenty years in prison. He looked closely at some of the other prisoners in the room. They all had the same haunted look that he was probably wearing himself.

They were faces that few got to see, *certainly not the college kids I'll be up against,* he thought. They were faces that needed painting.

The End

To read about John Hoskison's own experience of prison please read the bestselling book
Inside – One Man's Experience of Prison.

To find out about his experiences playing the PGA European Golf Tour read the bestselling golf biography
No Hiding in The Open

Made in the USA
San Bernardino, CA
19 December 2013